SO-AZZ-038

Hadn't Gene already indicated that he was an uncaring playboy... the kind of man who took what he wanted simply because his money and position allowed him to be as mercenary as he liked?

Yet here Rose was in his isolated sanctuary on a remote Scottish island miles away from anywhere civilized, and until the boatman met her tomorrow to take her back to the mainland, she had to make the best of things. She'd sleep a whole lot better tonight if she didn't antagonize the man.

But despite all of that, she couldn't help recalling that crazily unreal moment when her gaze had locked with Gene's and molten desire had made her feel frighteningly weak. For a shocking instant, there was the urge to abandon all reason and surrender to the wild and wanton nature of it... How was any sane person able to explain such a thing?

Seven Sexy Sins

The *true* taste of temptation!

From greed to gluttony, lust to envy, these
fabulous stories explore what seven sexy sins
mean in the twenty-first century!

Whether pride goes before a fall,
or wrath leads to passion that consumes entirely,
one thing is certain...the road to true love
has never been more enticing!

So you decide:

How can it be a sin when it feels so good?

Sloth—Cathy Williams

Lust—Dani Collins

Pride—Kim Lawrence

Gluttony—Maggie Cox

Greed—Sara Craven

Wrath—Maya Blake

Envy—Annie West

Seven titles by some of
our most treasured and exciting authors!

Maggie Cox

A Taste of Sin

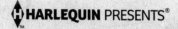
HARLEQUIN PRESENTS®

If you purchased this book without a cover you should be aware
that this book is stolen property. It was reported as "unsold and
destroyed" to the publisher, and neither the author nor the
publisher has received any payment for this "stripped book."

ISBN-13: 978-0-373-13355-0

A Taste of Sin

First North American publication 2015

Copyright © 2015 by Maggie Cox

Recycling programs
for this product may
not exist in your area.

All rights reserved. Except for use in any review, the reproduction or
utilization of this work in whole or in part in any form by any electronic,
mechanical or other means, now known or hereinafter invented, including
xerography, photocopying and recording, or in any information storage
or retrieval system, is forbidden without the written permission of the
publisher, Harlequin Enterprises Limited, 225 Duncan Mill Road,
Don Mills, Ontario M3B 3K9, Canada.

This is a work of fiction. Names, characters, places and incidents are
either the product of the author's imagination or are used fictitiously,
and any resemblance to actual persons, living or dead, business
establishments, events or locales is entirely coincidental.

This edition published by arrangement with Harlequin Books S.A.

For questions and comments about the quality of this book,
please contact us at CustomerService@Harlequin.com.

® and TM are trademarks of Harlequin Enterprises Limited or its
corporate affiliates. Trademarks indicated with ® are registered in the
United States Patent and Trademark Office, the Canadian Intellectual
Property Office and in other countries.

HARLEQUIN®
www.Harlequin.com

Printed in U.S.A.

Maggie Cox is passionate about stories that can uplift and transport people out of their daily worries to a more magical place, be they romance novels or fairy tales. What people want most, she believes, is true connection. She feels blessed to be married to a lovely man who never fails to make her laugh, and has two beautiful sons and two much loved grandchildren.

Books by Maggie Cox

Harlequin Presents

A Rule Worth Breaking
The Man She Can't Forget
The Tycoon's Delicious Distraction
In Petrakis's Power
What His Money Can't Hide
The Lost Wife
The Brooding Stranger
Mistress, Mother...Wife?
Surrender to Her Spanish Husband
The Buenos Aires Marriage Deal

The Powerful and the Pure
Distracted by Her Virtue

A Deal with the Devil
A Devilishly Dark Deal

One Night In...
One Desert Night

British Bachelors
Secretary by Day, Mistress by Night

Visit the Author Profile page
at Harlequin.com for more titles.

To Karen Middlemiss at the MS Therapy Centre.
Whenever we speak you help me
make peace with this condition and remind me
that life is for living whatever our challenge.
With love and blessings, Maggie

CHAPTER ONE

ROSE WAS STANDING by the window, mesmerised by the steady rain that hadn't let up all morning, when a gleaming black Mercedes drew up in front of the antiques shop and effortlessly glided to a stop.

It was just like a scene from a movie and she was immediately riveted. Inside her chest her heart thumped hard, because she knew it was the visitor she'd nervously been anticipating... *Eugene Bonnaire.*

Even the name gave her chills. He was one of the country's wealthiest restaurateurs, with an uncompromising reputation for getting what he wanted, and when Rose's boss, Philip, had put the beautiful Thames-side antiques shop he owned up for sale the businessman had wasted no time in declaring his interest.

Not for the first time that morning she wished Philip could be there alongside her, but sadly his already failing health had deteriorated and he was now in hospital. In his absence, he had asked Rose to handle the property's sale on his behalf.

The responsibility was a bittersweet one. Not just because he was ill, and she feared he might not recover, but because she'd nurtured a secret hope to take over the business herself one day. Having spent ten enjoyable years working with Philip, and training as a dealer, she'd honestly grown to love the place. Consequently, she wasn't predisposed to warming to their potential buyer.

Her first glimpse of the man, after his chauffeur had opened his door and he'd stepped out into the rain, was of a pair of classy Italian brogues, followed by a flawless charcoal suit that was no less than stunningly perfect. Rose caught her breath. As soon as she saw his arrestingly sculpted features, the cut-glass jaw and crystalline blue eyes that were frequently described by the press as 'unflinchingly piercing', she had the disturbing sense that she was coming face to face with her greatest fear and—*inexplicably*—her greatest desire...

She irritably chided herself for the thought. Snapping out of the near trance she'd fallen into watching him, she smoothed her hands down her smart navy dress and made herself walk calmly to the door. It was then she saw that the businessman's height dwarfed hers.

Lifting her head to gaze up at him, she said, 'Eugene Bonnaire? Please come in. I'm Mr Houghton's assistant—Rose Heathcote. I've been asked to conduct the meeting with you on Mr Houghton's behalf.'

The handsome Frenchman stepped inside. Charmingly polite, he shook Rose's hand with a slight bow of his head and she immediately sensed the reined-in strength he exuded.

'I am delighted to meet you, Miss Heathcote. But I

have to confess I was sorry to hear that your boss has been taken ill. Might I ask how he is?'

Before answering, Rose pulled the door shut behind him and adjusted the sign that hung inside the glass to read 'closed'. She was glad of the chance to compose herself before she turned round again. Not only had his firm handshake made her far too aware of him as a man, but the deep bass timbre of his arrestingly attractive voice made her skin feel as though he'd brushed it with gossamer. She prayed that the blood that had heatedly rushed into her face didn't too obviously reveal the fact…

'I wish I could say he was a little better, but the doctors tell me it's going to be a while before we see any improvement.'

'*C'est la vie*. It is the way of things…but I wish him well.'

'Thank you. I'll tell him you said so. Anyway, would you like to come with me into the office, Mr Bonnaire, and we can start our meeting?'

'Before we discuss anything I would like you to show me round the building, Miss Heathcote. After all, that is the reason I am here.'

Although there was a faultlessly charming smile on his lips to accompany this statement, Rose realised that here was a man who wouldn't be diverted by small talk, however polite and concerned. Nothing would take precedence over pursuing his goals, and his goal today was clearly deciding whether he wanted to buy the antiques shop or not…

'Of course,' she replied. 'It will be my pleasure.'

Rose led him upstairs to one of the three spacious rooms that, although elegantly arranged, were stacked to the rafters with a mixture of antiques and collectables. The air smelled faintly musty because there was a generous amount of furniture on display, although it was tempered somewhat by the scent of beeswax.

While the sound of the rain against the leaded windows made for a cosy ambience it was a little chilly too, and the dress she wore was sleeveless. Wishing she'd collected her cardigan from the office, she briskly rubbed her arms to warm them.

'The rooms are generously sized, considering it's such an old building,' she remarked, 'which is why we can house so many antiques. I hope you like what you see, Mr Bonnaire.'

Looking faintly amused, her visitor lifted his gaze.

Rose privately attested to spending the most electrifying few seconds of her life as her glance met his. It struck her that she could have chosen her words better. Not in a million years would she invite a man like Eugene Bonnaire to look at her. Did he think that she *would?* He had a reputation for liking exceptionally beautiful women, and Rose knew she was a long way from being in that particular category.

'So far...I like what I see very much, Miss Heathcote,' he answered, not moving his gaze.

Now she really *did* feel hot and bothered. 'I'm... I'm glad. Take as much time as you want, looking over things.'

'Trust me, I will do exactly that.'

'Good.'

Hastily averting her glance, she crossed her arms over her chest, not wanting to draw any more attention. But it wasn't long before she found herself surreptitiously observing him as he walked round, his keen-eyed gaze carefully examining the layout and proportions of the room, every so often dropping down into a crouch to examine the durability and condition of the timbered walls and crevices. It was fascinating to watch him stroking his large but slim hands over the wood and occasionally tapping it with his knuckles.

Whilst Rose understood that it was important the man knew what he would be getting for his investment, he didn't give the impression that the room's contents interested him at all, and she began to be concerned. Philip had told her it was imperative he sell the business as a going concern, because his poor health meant that he now had to retire, as well as pay for his aftercare when he left the hospital.

He had added sadly, 'I'm afraid that pensions aren't worth a light these days…'

The weight of the responsibility she'd taken on in agreeing to make the sale for him hit Rose even harder.

She was still frowning when the preoccupied Frenchman pivoted and remarked, 'Forgive me, but I saw you shiver a couple of times. Are you cold? Perhaps you'd like to go and get your jacket, Rose?'

Even as he asked another small shiver ran up her spine. But it wasn't due to the less than comfortable temperature…it was because it had sounded disturbingly intimate when he'd used her name.

Last night, ahead of her interview with him, she had

looked up Eugene Bonnaire on the internet, and as well as reading about the numerous plaudits he had earned in his career thus far she had also learned that he could be quite ruthless in his dealings and had an insatiable appetite for success. He was cited as a man who went after the very best of everything, no matter what the cost, and his penchant for stunning women suggested he was quite the playboy.

Rose knew she couldn't afford to let her guard down round him for an instant. She didn't want to be persuaded to agree to the sale of the business against her better judgement just because he was so attractive.

Deciding that she couldn't and *wouldn't* let that happen—she knew from bitter experience the danger that men like him could pose—she unwaveringly returned his gaze and said, 'I think I *will* go and get my cardigan. If you want to look at the other rooms on this floor, be my guest. I'll be back in a minute.'

With a polite but inarguably *knowing* nod, Eugene Bonnaire glanced away.

A short while later she returned upstairs to find that he'd gone into the furthest room at the back. This was where the more valuable items were displayed and where jewellery was housed behind secure custom-made glass cabinets. Much to Rose's surprise, she found Eugene staring transfixed into one of the cabinets and wondered if she'd misjudged him. Maybe he *did* admire some of the artefacts and maybe he *would* buy the business as well as the building?

She couldn't help but smile as she stepped up beside him, curious to see what he was examining so avidly.

When she saw that he was staring at the exquisite pearl and diamond ring from the nineteenth century that was the centrepiece of the display, her curiosity was even more piqued.

'It's pretty, isn't it?' she commented.

'Yes, it is. It looks very similar to the ring my father bought my mother when their business first started to take off.' He was lost in thought for a moment. Then, with a heartfelt sigh, he turned towards her. 'But the pearls and the diamonds weren't real. They were just costume jewellery... He couldn't afford to buy her anything expensive back then.'

There was definitely a glimmer of pain in his eyes as he related this, and Rose found herself warming to him probably more than was wise, because he suddenly seemed oddly vulnerable.

'I'm sure your mum loved the ring just as much as if it were the genuine article. Surely it's what it represented, not how much it cost?' When Eugene failed to comment, and turned back to examine the jewel broodingly, she said softly, 'You might be interested to know that this ring was given to a girl who was a nurse in the Crimean War by the grateful family of a wounded soldier.'

His crystal blue gaze meandered interestedly across her features. Then he gazed deeply into her eyes. Rose's mouth went dry as a sun-bleached plain... She was glad she was wearing her navy wool cardigan so he wouldn't see her shiver again.

'Every picture tells a story, so they say,' he mused. 'No doubt it's the same for jewellery. But let me ask you this: do you think the nurse who was gifted it was very pretty and the wounded soldier a handsome officer?'

The roguish twinkle that accompanied his question took her by surprise and all but made Rose's knees buckle. Flooded with heat, she congratulated herself on quickly regaining her equilibrium and not glancing away too soon. Instead, she made herself steadily hold his gaze and her lips curved in a gentle smile.

'Whether he was handsome or not, shortly after they met he died from his wounds. It's a terribly sad story, isn't it? Whether the two of them had feelings for each other we can only wonder, but the giving of the ring was documented in the soldier's family archives. That's how we were able to trace its provenance.'

'I am guessing that you like to imagine the couple *did* have feelings for each other, Rose.' Eugene's expression was suddenly intense.

Feeling strangely as if she was under siege, she shrugged. 'Why not? Who could begrudge them the little bit of happiness they may have had in the midst of such a terrible situation? But the truth is we'll never know what really happened.'

What Rose *did* know was that she had to engineer some space between her and Eugene. She might at one point have felt a chill, but now she was definitely warmer...*too* warm.

'If you've finished having a look round up here we should go downstairs and have that meeting...don't you think?'

'I agree. Perhaps you could make us some coffee?'

'Of course… How do you take it?'

'How do you *think* I might take it, Rose? Humour me.'

If his tactic was to disarm her and lull her into a false sense of security because he'd decided to be playful, Rose couldn't deny that on another day she might have succumbed to his charm. After all, what woman *wouldn't* feel flattered by his exclusive attention? But today she wouldn't be so easily swayed. Not when she had an important task to fulfil. She had to sell the antiques shop on her boss's behalf and secure the very best deal she could. Nothing could distract her from that goal.

Leading the way back downstairs, in an attempt to let Eugene see that she wasn't rattled by his friendly repartee, she breezily threw over her shoulder, 'Okay, then. I'm guessing you probably like it strong and black. But I'm also guessing you like a couple of spoons of sugar to sweeten it. Am I right?'

'I'm impressed. But be careful not to assume you know what I like in any other respect, Rose… You might find that you've bitten off a little bit more than you can chew.'

Even though she'd heard a smile in his voice, Rose didn't doubt the comment carried a warning. No man became as successful as Eugene Bonnaire without carefully assessing anyone who might put obstacles in the way of him getting what he wanted…

When she returned to the office with the tray of coffee she'd made Eugene had his back to her, and she couldn't help but let her gaze linger for a moment on the impres-

sive breadth of his shoulders. In the better lit room she
also saw that his hair was a rich dark brown, with dulled
gold lights glinting here and there.

As if that wasn't enough to capture her attention, the
scent of his classy cologne drifted beguilingly on the
air and made her insides turn over. With the tip of her
tongue she moistened her suddenly dry lips and placed
the tray on the gracious Victorian desk in front of him.
Then she walked round to the beautifully carved chair
that her boss usually occupied.

Coming face to face with Eugene's features again
was not something any woman with a pulse would soon
forget… He was chisel-jawed and handsome as a Mi-
chelangelo sculpture. But she was perturbed when she
saw that his dazzling blue eyes didn't seem as warm
as they had upstairs, when she'd met his gaze over the
jewellery cabinet and he'd shared that touching story
about the fake pearl and diamond ring his father had
bought his mother.

In fact, as they swept over her they brought to mind
a once sunlit ocean frozen under ice. A little alarmed,
Rose sensed hot colour flooding into her cheeks. *Was
he assessing the way she looked?*

Having never considered herself a beauty, she was
painfully disconcerted at being scrutinised by the businessman so penetratingly. Friends had often remarked
that her best features were her eyes and her cheekbones,
but other than that she knew she was quite ordinary.
Disturbed that she should waste even a second fretting
over what the man's opinion of her might be her instinct
was to be doubly wary of him.

But the restaurateur's carved lips curved in another disconcerting smile. 'Would you like to pour the coffee for us? Then we can proceed. I have a particularly heavy schedule today, and would like to settle our business as quickly as possible.'

'You sound as though you've made a decision?'

'I have. Having seen the interior of the building, I'd like to make you an offer.'

Straight away Rose noted that he'd said 'the building'—not the antiques business. Her stomach plunged like a stone.

'I'd really like to tie up the sale of the property today,' he added smoothly, bringing his hands together with his long fingers forming a steeple.

His words suggested it was a given that she would agree to the sale. Maybe he didn't think she could possibly refuse him because she was only standing in for the owner? Perhaps he imagined his wealth and status would intimidate her?

If she was right, then his arrogance beggared belief. Biting her lip, she decided to delay commenting and garner her thoughts.

Reaching for the cafetière, she carefully poured out his coffee. 'It's two sugars, isn't it?' she checked, aware that his intense gaze was closely surveying everything she did and resenting it mightily.

'That's right.'

Passing him the beverage, Rose made a particular point of *not* meeting his gaze. After pouring her own drink she sat down, but in truth she knew any hopes she might have had of remaining calm throughout the meeting had fled as soon as her glance had encountered the Frenchman's…

'Can I just clarify something? You said that you wanted to tie up the sale of "the property" today?'

'That's correct'

'Forgive me, but I thought my boss had made it clear that he wanted to sell the business as a going concern, Mr Bonnaire? You can't separate it from the property and just purchase the building. Do I take it that you're not interested in running the antiques shop at all?'

'That's right, Rose—but, please, call me Gene. You may or may not know, but I already run a very successful worldwide restaurant business and I'd like to install one of my most prestigious restaurants here. The location is perfect. And, although I do also have other successful businesses, to be frank with you I'm afraid that antiques don't interest me in the slightest. I'm sure you must have learned from your boss that people just aren't as interested in them these days as they used to be. Anyone in business wants to make money. No interest in the product, equals no profit. Isn't that the reason why he wants to sell?'

Rose felt as if her face had suddenly been seared by an iron. She was both embarrassed and furious. 'You don't have to be so brutal—'

'Business *is* brutal, *ma chère*…make no mistake about that.'

'Well, Philip is selling because he's ill and no longer has the energy to run the business. This antiques shop has always been his pride and joy, and if he was well I can assure you it wouldn't be up for sale at all.'

It was Gene's turn to sigh. 'But I'm guessing the fact is, due to his poor health, he's decided to take the opportunity to make as much money as he can on his asset while he is still in a position to do so. Is that not so?'

She flushed again, and twisted her hands in her lap to still their trembling. She couldn't make a proper decision about anything if her emotions got in the way. But Gene, as he seemed to prefer being called, had guessed right. Because of his failing health Philip *needed* to make this sale. But she knew that he'd fervently hoped to sell the business along with the building, and if Rose didn't manage to do that for him then she would have failed the man who was not just her boss and mentor, but who had been her father's dearest friend…

She came to the only decision that could possibly be right. Now calmer, she met the Frenchman's gaze across the desk. 'It's true that Mr Houghton needs to make this sale, Mr Bonnaire—Gene—but, since you've just admitted that antiques don't interest you in the slightest, and that you're not interested in running the business and only want the building, I'm afraid I can't agree to sell it to you. It just wouldn't be right. I realise it's not the decision you hoped for, but I'm sorry. I hope you understand?'

'No. I do *not* understand. I have told you that it's the building I'm interested in and I'm willing to pay what I know to be the going rate for the property…no question. How many interested buyers has your boss seen since he put the shop up for sale?'

Gene Bonnaire's glare was steely.

'In the current economic climate my guess is not

many… Maybe I'm the only one? If I were you, Rose, I would take my offer on your employer's behalf and congratulate yourself. Trust me…the only regret he would have is if you should be foolish enough to turn me down. Do you *really* want to put yourself in such an untenable position and lose the faith and trust he has obviously accorded you?'

As a helpless tide of defensive anger surged through her Rose set her eyes on the man she now considered to be not quite so charming. He might not be as heartless as she'd first thought—the story about the fake pearl and diamond ring his father had bought his mother demonstrated that he had the capacity to feel things deeply—but she knew that he was determined to secure the desirable Thames-side building at all costs. And he was plainly willing to risk Rose not liking him if he became too insistent.

'I think you've said quite enough, Mr Bonnaire. I've given you my decision and you're just going to have to accept it.'

'Is that so? Do you imagine that any businessman or woman worth their salt who is determined to seal a deal should give up so easily merely because you tell them that they *should*?'

His tone was sardonic, and Gene's glance swept over Rose as if she was a foolish little girl.

Swallowing down her fury that anybody could be so reprehensible, she stiffly folded her arms. 'I wouldn't dream of advising anyone what's best for them, because I clearly don't know. I'm not a businesswoman… I'm an antiques dealer. However, I *do* know my boss

Philip, and how much this antiques business means to him. He's impressed upon me more than once that he wants to sell it as a going concern, so I would be failing in my duty if I didn't adhere to that. On his behalf, I thank you for your interest but our meeting is over. I'll see you to the door.'

'Not so fast.'

As he rose immediately to his feet it wasn't hard for Rose to detect that Gene Bonnaire was more than a little thrown off balance by her refusal to sell. He was holding on to his temper by a thread.

The expensive cologne he wore again stirred the air, reminding her that the moneyed and elite world he inhabited was light years away from hers and that he hadn't expected an argument. But on this occasion, Rose was determined to stand her ground…

'Look, I didn't come here to waste my time or yours,' he went on. 'I came here for one reason and one reason only: to purchase a listed building that I understood was up for sale. If you won't sell the premises to me then perhaps you'd reconsider your decision if I agree to purchase the antiques as well? I don't doubt some of them might be valuable to an ardent collector.'

The comment was hardly encouraging. He might just as well have referred to the collector as misguided rather than ardent. Rose didn't have to guess how appalled Philip would be if he knew that Gene didn't want to purchase the antiques for their beauty and historical significance, or even because he might be considering continuing the business after all, but only because he was thinking about their monetary worth.

'Indeed, some of them are extremely valuable,' she confirmed. 'But unfortunately your remark illustrates to me exactly what you asserted earlier...you have no interest whatsoever in antiques. That being the case, I'm not inclined to consider your offer any further, Mr Bonnaire.'

Extracting a leather wallet from the inside pocket of the impeccably tailored jacket he wore, the businessman took out a card and threw it down onto the desk. The blue eyes that Rose had noted could be icy had turned even more glacial.

'When you've had some time to think things over—meaning when you can make a far less *emotional* decision about the matter, Rose—I don't doubt you'll want to get in touch with me to discuss a sale. In the meantime, I'll say *au revoir.*'

As he spoke Rose found herself yet again uncomfortably captured by his mocking glance, and she thanked her lucky stars that the man was going. Yet as her gaze followed him to the door in truth she didn't know whether or not to be pleased she'd stood her ground—whether the decision she'd made was the right one or not...

Back in his Mayfair office, after the tedious round of meetings he'd chaired that afternoon, Gene asked his secretary to get him some coffee and sank down into his high-backed leather chair to mull over the day's events. He didn't think he had ever felt more irritable and out of sorts, and it was all down to his offer being refused on that damn property.

He'd admired the architecture of the Thames-side building for years, and had often thought it would make the most fantastic restaurant should he buy it. He didn't envisage it as an addition to the more commercial restaurants he already owned, but saw it as the kind of exclusive place that the glitterati liked to frequent. Just like the two esteemed establishments he owned in New York and Paris.

Recalling his meeting with Rose Heathcote, Gene mused that it was beyond his understanding how she couldn't see what a gold-edged opportunity to capitalise on his assets he had given her boss. Most people would have ripped his arm off to take it. But one thing had become eminently clear to him… Just as she had said, Rose was no businesswoman. Her attitude had really irked him. Especially when he'd seen that she wasn't going to be easily influenced by any amount of charm he might utilise. Yet part of him admired the brunette for her determination to stand firm even though he knew she was wrong.

And there was something else about her that had caught his attention. *She had the most startlingly beautiful violet eyes.* Her glossy black hair and ivory-coloured skin made them even more captivating. The passion he'd seen in their mesmerising depths had intrigued him and made him want to get to know her, even though she'd denied him the chance to purchase the property. But, as was his modus operandi when faced with situations or outcomes he didn't like, Gene knew he would immediately work to turn it to his advantage.

Yes…he would step right back into the breach and

make his purchase of the building a foregone conclusion. He wouldn't be satisfied until it was his. Rose could take a couple of days' sober reflection on what a mistake she'd made in turning him down, then Gene would get back to her with an offer that he knew her boss simply *couldn't* refuse.

If he could have some more time with her and assure her that he was respectful of the gracious building's admirable history, had always admired it and only sought to elevate it by housing his restaurant there, he didn't doubt he could persuade her to convince Philip Houghton that selling the building to one of the country's richest entrepreneurs wasn't just a good idea…it was the *only* one that would take it off his hands and make him enough money to see him right for the rest of his life.

But just then, somewhere deep inside him, Gene couldn't help feeling disturbed that he'd so easily dismissed the other man's welfare in the belief that money was the answer to his problems. Even his parents had counselled him on that once.

'Son, you can't always fix someone's pain by throwing money at the problem. No amount of money or good fortune made it any easier for us to endure the devastation of your sister's death. Don't forget that.'

The memory jolted him, and for a few disturbing seconds he felt as if a grenade had been thrown into the room. But now wasn't the time to reflect on how much his sister's death had nearly broken him…

He squared his shoulders. He and his parents saw life very differently. Gene saw practical solutions to adversity while they succumbed to their emotions and

allowed their feelings to dictate how they responded…
The idea of behaving in the same way was anathema
to him. He'd heard his parents' stories about their poor
upbringings, how their own parents and siblings had
suffered terribly when there hadn't been the means to
put food on the table or to have adequate heat and light,
and how many nights they had gone to bed hungry…
From a tender age he'd intuited how essential it was to
have money, and as he'd grown older, having discovered
that he had a talent for making it with ease, he wasn't
about to relinquish it—not for *anyone*.

Pleased that he'd come up with a plan to help him
win the beautiful old property—a plan he was convinced would work because he never, *never* entertained
the possibility of failure—Gene got to his feet, straightened his tie and strode out through the door.

Stopping at the desk of his blonde, statuesque secretary, Simone, whose cousin was an up-and-coming Parisian designer—and frankly that was why he'd given
her the job…because it always paid to utilise his assets—he flashed her a warmer smile than usual and
said, 'Forget the coffee, *ma chère,* and book me a table
for dinner at my club for eight o'clock.'

'Will you be taking a guest with you, Mr Bonnaire?'

'No, Simone. Not tonight.'

'Then I will ring the *maître d'* straight away and arrange for you to have your favourite table.'

'Thank you.'

'You are most welcome. It always makes me glad
when I can do something to please you and make your
life a little easier.'

The woman's glossy pink lips curved in a smile that was definitely inviting.

Gene's fleetingly good mood instantly vanished. Scowling, he said, 'In that case you won't mind doing some overtime tonight, will you? I've left a "to do" list on my desk for you. Goodnight, Simone. I will see you in the morning.'

He was more irritated than usual with the blonde's obsequious manner. She hadn't been working for him for very long, but he didn't need to be a genius to know that she was only too aware of how to use *her* best assets…especially as she clearly thought it was only a matter of time before he would bed her… Just yesterday he had overheard her stating the fact, not very discreetly, to someone on her mobile.

Waiting impatiently for the elevator to arrive, he muttered savagely beneath his breath, 'God save me from predatory women!'

CHAPTER TWO

LONG AFTER HER MEETING, and still stinging from her encounter with the mercurial force of nature that was Gene Bonnaire, Rose couldn't help but be interested in what drove the man to be the way he was. He clearly hadn't liked her decision not to sell the shop to him. Her refusal had really grated on him, because he obviously wasn't used to being denied when he'd set his sights on something that he wanted.

Knowing that he was a restaurateur, and that he wanted the building for one of his establishments, that night she went home and did some more research.

Rose discovered that Gene was one of the richest men in Europe and had made his fortune by turning a once small French restaurant in East London called Mangez Bien into a well-known chain that had spread across the globe. The original restaurant had been owned by Gene's parents. They were both French immigrants, who'd settled in London when they were young and had turned their love of cooking and food into owning a much loved eatery that had been patronised by a devoted local clientele.

By the time their son had turned seventeen, so the story went, he was already a fine chef whose ambitions far exceeded his parents' own. He had progressed from being Head Chef at one of London's finest hotels to becoming an astute entrepreneur who had started to establish restaurants of his own. But as he'd begun to build an empire of affordable French restaurants he had also acquired a reputation for being quite ruthless in his business dealings.

Rose already knew he didn't like being denied...

Leaning back in her chair, she studied the photograph that her computer had helpfully supplied. It had been taken at a prestigious awards ceremony in LA, and even though the picture of him couldn't help but be flattering, to her mind it didn't depict any pleasure at his being at the event, nor at having received an award. Instead, the man's immense dissatisfaction was clear. It emanated from Gene's steely blue eyes in forbidding icy waves...

He doesn't look even remotely pleased, she mused. And he was probably even less pleased since she'd turned down his offer.

The headline of the article onscreen read, *The man who has everything once again strikes gold.*

'Hmph,' Rose muttered out loud. 'That doesn't mean that any of what he's got makes him happy. *Something* must be bugging him...something he doesn't like to talk about.'

Was it anything to do with his father not being able to afford a *real* diamond and pearl ring for his mother in the early days when they were starting to establish their business? Why else had he told Rose that it was only costume jewellery? Had it made him feel insecure? She remembered the flicker of pain that had accompanied his remark. But surely he wasn't still burdened by the memory? Was he sad that once upon a time his parents had struggled...that not everything had been as easy for them as it had for their son?

Wearily dragging her fingers through her pixie cut short hair, she sighed. Why was Gene Bonnaire at the forefront of her thoughts when she still had to face her boss and tell him that she'd turned down the Frenchman's offer?

She would have done anything to spare him the disappointment and distress the news would undoubtedly bring him, and could only hope he would see that her motivation had been to do what was right by him. After all, he'd been there for her when her father had passed away, staying by his bedside with Rose until he breathed his last breath... The last thing he needed now, when he was so ill, was to be put under pressure to sell the antiques shop to someone who didn't have the first idea about what it meant to him...

Switching off her computer, she stood up and stretched. Annoyed that she'd wasted even more time thinking about Gene Bonnaire, she went into her living room to collect the book she'd been reading. It was a hefty tome all about the Aztecs, with a fascinating chapter on the magnificent jewellery worn by the emperors. There had recently been a momentous find in northern Mexico, and straight away it had fuelled Rose's interest. She'd have loved to go and see the treasure that the archaeologists had uncovered, but she'd have to wait until it finally went on display in a prestigious gallery or museum.

Going to bed, she fell asleep with the book on her chest and dreamt disturbingly of an Aztec emperor who uncannily resembled Gene Bonnaire...

Just like an addict, desperate to buy his next fix, Gene sat in the café across the street from the antiques store and couldn't turn his mind to anything else other than fulfilling his desire to own the gracious building he was staring at... The coffee he'd ordered had long gone cold as he restlessly contemplated going in and demanding that Rose Heathcote came to her senses and accepted the offer he'd made.

It had been three days since their meeting, and no phone call had been forthcoming to tell him that she'd had second thoughts. Maybe her boss had had a better offer from someone else? The very idea made him feel nauseous. He wanted that building as much as he wanted his next breath, and he deplored the notion that he might not get it.

Glancing down at his Rolex, he saw that he'd been sitting in the café for nigh on half an hour, hoping to catch Rose unawares. Catching someone off-guard often paid dividends, he'd found. If he'd seen her then he would have asked her out to dinner, so that they could talk amicably outside of work and get to know each other a little better. If he was able to get her to trust him then he didn't doubt he could persuade her to sell the building to him.

But she hadn't stepped outside even once, and in

truth he was taking an unnecessary risk, sitting in the café in front of the window. Any minute now the paparazzi might turn up—and that really *would* ruin his day, because they were frequently on a mission to expose him as ruthless and uncaring...

Even in the early days, when he'd started to have some success, he'd realised there were more people in the world who were jealous of his achievements rather than pleased. More to the point, they were jealous of his *wealth*... Knowing that, he knew the press was more than eager to take him down a peg or two—no doubt so that their readers could feel a bit better about their own lives.

Suddenly impatient, he glanced upwards at the now darkening skies. Any moment now it would start to rain. He shouldn't waste any more time sitting there, waiting for inspiration to dawn about what he should do. He'd never been someone who *waited* for opportunity to strike. Gene made his own opportunities.

His gaze settled on the old building again. The name of the shop was The Hidden Diamond, and to be honest he thought it a little trite. After all, he reasoned, if it was hidden then what use was it to anybody? Diamonds should be displayed to denote their owner's wealth... not hidden away.

With a jaundiced sigh he got to his feet. The promised rain began to splatter the pavement. He was done with waiting. He was going into the shop to present Rose with a more persuasive offer. If she really cared so much about helping her boss then she ought to be relieved he was giving her a second bite of the cherry...

* * *

Rose was finishing up her bookwork when she heard the doorbell chime. Hurriedly toeing on her maroon leather flats, she tucked her cream silk blouse more securely into the waistband of her smart black skirt and left the office to deal with what she assumed was a late customer.

She should have closed up shop half an hour ago, but she'd been so immersed in cataloguing the dwindling monthly sales and wishing they were better that she hadn't noticed the time.

Her lips automatically curved into a smile, but the gesture immediately melted away when she saw that her late caller wasn't the customer she'd envisaged but Gene Bonnaire. She stared. What was *he* doing here? Forgoing a suit, he was dressed casually today, in jeans and a dove-grey T-shirt beneath a tailored black jacket. But he was no less formidable. It was raining outside, she saw, and the shoulders of his jacket glistened with moisture—as did his hair.

'Do you usually stay open this late?' he asked, clearly opting to dispense with any social niceties.

Tensing, Rose found herself caught in the crystalline spotlight of his disquieting blue gaze. 'Not usually no. But I was busy doing some bookwork and didn't notice the time. What can I do for you, Mr Bonnaire? If you were hoping to persuade me to change my mind about your offer then I'm sorry. I wouldn't want you to waste your time.'

'Don't be sorry. Just let me have a few minutes with you to talk things over.'

'To what end?'

'Why don't we sit down and I'll tell you?'

Rose arched an eyebrow. 'Like I said, I gave you my decision and I see no reason in discussing it any further.' When Gene scowled she got the distinct impression that he was having considerable trouble remaining calm. His next words confirmed it.

'You really have no idea about business, do you, Rose? I'd like to know why your boss, Philip Houghton, has such faith in you… Perhaps you'd enlighten me?'

Now Rose had trouble holding on to her own temper, and she had no hesitation in replying passionately, 'Because I care about him—that's why! I have no ulterior motive other than that I want what's best for him. And what's best for him is to sell the antiques business as a going concern, to someone who will love it as much as he does.'

'That's a nice thought…but hardly a realistic one.'

'Did you come here just to tell me how inept you think I am, Mr Bonnaire?' Incensed, she folded her arms. 'Because if it makes you feel any better, then you should know that I've had sleepless nights about the whole thing. It would be very easy to take your offer to my boss and tell him that he'd be lucky to get another one half as good—remind him that the antiques trade isn't what it used to be and he should just take what he can while the going's good. But I couldn't be so cruel. Not when I know how much the business means to him. If he was just interested in selling a beautiful period building in a very desirable area then he would have done so. But he wants the business to continue… What

do you think he'd say if I accepted your offer and then
told him you weren't remotely interested in antiques?'

Gene looked thoughtful. Then he smiled. 'I think
he'd probably feel that he can't be sentimental about it.
At the end of the day, if he believes that his poor health
will prohibit his return to work, no doubt he will need
the money to help pay for his care. Surely that's the
priority here?'

What he said made perfect sense and, suddenly unsure, Rose felt tears of frustration surge into her eyes.

Gene all but covered the distance between them in
less than a couple of strides, and as before the air stirred
hypnotically with the exotic scent of his expensive cologne.

'You're upset. Is there anything I can do? Why don't
we go into the office and I'll get you a cup of tea?'

'I don't want tea. All I want is… All I want is for
you to go away!' Her outburst sounded embarrassingly
childish even to her own ears… *So much for keeping
her composure.* Rose wanted the ground to open up
and swallow her.

But the man in front of her didn't go away. He didn't
even look remotely put out. The dazzling blue eyes that
she knew could turn forbiddingly cold when he was
angry were now inexplicably warm…*tender*, even. He
lifted his hand to touch her arm gently. Her heart thud-
ded quietly as she felt his smooth skin brush against
her own.

'Your boss gave you a tough job when he asked you
to sell the business for him, Rose—perhaps *too* tough.
I don't mean this as a criticism, but I can see that it's

not where your skills lie… I've already learned that it's the *job* you love—being with the artefacts and learning about their history. More than that, you like discovering the personal stories behind them. You're a *people* person, Rose…not a businesswoman.'

She realised the man had an almost uncanny knack of knowing what a person was about. But she didn't want to let him see even for a second that his astute insight perturbed her. Surely Gene Bonnaire had enough advantages without her giving him any more…namely the fact that she could so easily warm to him, when everything in her told her it would be a mistake that would undoubtedly cost her dear…

'That might be the case, and I *know* my forte isn't in the world of business—I told you that before. But my love of antiques and understanding what they mean to people also makes me understand why my boss, Philip, wants to sell the business as a going concern. I think it means even more to him since he's become ill. He's taught me so much about the trade, and that's why I want to get the best deal for him.'

'That's also why you should give me a little bit more of your time and listen to what I have to say, Rose.'

'Why? Are you going to tell me that you've decided to take on the business after all?'

Gene was already shaking his head. 'No. I'm sorry I have to disappoint you, but I won't be getting involved in that side of things. I haven't changed my mind about that.'

'Then how can I possibly be interested in listening any more to what you have to say, Mr Bonnaire?'

'If you'd do me the courtesy of having dinner with me tonight, I'll explain.'

Even as she guessed that most women would be surprised and pleased by such an invitation—not to mention immensely flattered—Rose defiantly lifted her chin to indicate that she wasn't one of them. 'Thank you, but I'm going to have to decline.'

'You have a previous engagement?'

'No, but—'

'You don't want to hear what I have to say, even though it might be to your boss's advantage?'

'How can it *possibly* be to his advantage? You've already said that you're not interested in the business… that you only want the building.'

Gene Bonnaire's steely-eyed gaze didn't waver for so much as a second as he examined her, and it was easy to guess he'd hoped to have the upper hand.

'Like I said, Rose… Have dinner with me tonight and all will be explained.'

Prickling with unease, she sensed herself flush heatedly. 'You're just playing games—and I don't trust men who play games. If you have something to say that you know for a fact my boss will be interested in, then why don't you just come right out and say it?'

'Very well, then, although I'm sad that you won't agree to dinner, and just to reassure you, Rose, I'm not playing games. It's just that it has been my experience that all the best deals are made over a cordon bleu meal and a fine bottle of wine.'

One corner of the handsome Frenchman's mouth lifted in a smile that would make most women—young, old and in between—*ache* to be close to him in the most intimate way… And even though Rose was quite aware that he was using his charm to get what he wanted, she was hardly immune to the idea.

'Is that right? Well, I'm afraid that's not been *my* experience.'

'So you won't even take a risk and try it?'

Unable to glance away from his mesmerising gaze, she felt her breath hitch. 'No…I won't…'

But even as she refused a look of heated longing drifted across his irises and she sensed her resistance indisputably melting. Underneath their polite words, somehow a much more sensual conversation was taking place. Rose couldn't deny it. That impossibly irresistible look of Gene Bonnaire's was captivating her, stirring her own longing into life, and right then all she wanted to do was to fulfil it…

Gene moved to stand in front of her, his mesmerising blue eyes smouldering like simmering fires… In the next instant the businessman had firmly caught hold of her arm and pulled her against his chest.

Rose's blood pumped hard. All she could do was helplessly stare back at him. It was undeniable that he excited her, but his sheer physical presence disturbed her too. It only took a glance to see how supremely fit and strong he was.

Low-voiced, he murmured, 'God forgive me, but…'

The time that elapsed between his words and his next action was brief…*too* brief for her to stop him.

His urgent, initially demanding kiss stole her breath and made her sink against the hard wall of his chest.

Her senses were utterly besieged by him. And as his hot silken mouth moved over hers and became more and more seductive Rose didn't have the faintest inclination to end the passionate caress.

Then somehow it filtered through to her fogged brain just how dangerous her compliant actions were and she came hurtling back to her senses. Shocked and shaken, she freed herself from the Frenchman's embrace and wiped her hand over her already aching lips.

Staring back at him, she declared, 'Your arrogance, Mr Bonnaire, has to be seen to be believed! I don't know what you thought you were doing, but I think you'd better just leave.'

Her heart pumped even harder. The heat from his body and his velvet mouth had seared her indelibly, and she already knew she wasn't easily going to forget it.

'I didn't intend to kiss you, Rose, but somehow the desire overwhelmed me. I am as disturbed by it as you are. I apologise. If you really won't come to dinner with me then I can do no more than tell you about the amended deal I have come up with.'

He paused, as if to take a moment to straighten his thoughts. There was a slight crimson tint beneath his tan that bore out his declaration that desire had overwhelmed him. Rose didn't know what to make of it herself. She was just an ordinary girl, and he was—he was a living, breathing *Adonis*...

'I already know how much getting the best deal for your boss means to you, and I have spent quite some time thinking about how I can make that a reality for you both. This is my new offer.'

His hand dived into the inside pocket of his jacket and he drew out a slim sheet of paper. Unfolding it, he handed it to Rose.

Her jaw all but hit the floor when she saw how much he was prepared to pay for the privilege of owning the building. His initial offer had practically *doubled*. For dizzying moments she was literally lost for words.

'This amount of money can be a real life-changer for Philip, Rose. That being the case, why on earth would you turn down the opportunity to help make things better for him? If you were to persuade him to see the sense in selling to me, then I'm sure he would be nothing but relieved. If he accepted my offer then he would have the worry of the business off his hands and earn himself a more than healthy profit. No doubt *you* would be happy too, Rose, because his ill health would undoubtedly be restored and, last but not least, I don't deny *I* would be pleased, because I'd get the property I've long desired.'

'And the name of the game is always that you get what *you* want, isn't it, Mr Bonnaire? There's nothing altruistic about this scenario, is there? You don't give a fig about my employer's health, or whether I'm happy or not happy. Why *should* you? You know nothing about us! You've seen something you want and you'll do anything…pay *any* price…to get it. Isn't that how people like you operate?'

To Rose's consternation, he chuckled. It was a rich, gravelly sound that sent shivers running up and down her spine.

'*Touché*…you've got it in one. You're a bright woman…'

'Don't patronise me!'

Sighing, he folded his arms over his chest and studied her. 'I wouldn't dream of it. I'd much rather have you on my side than make you my enemy, Rose. By the way, your eyes are an *incredible* colour... I don't doubt you've been told that many times before. What's the shade? I'd say they were violet...'

Rose was hardly prepared for his remarks suddenly to become personal, even though he'd so passionately kissed her, and for several disturbing seconds it threw her. She could hardly think, let alone come back with a retort to put him in his place.

'The colour of my eyes is neither here nor there. This conversation is completely futile. Now, I really need to close the shop and you have to go.'

'Not yet. You haven't told me what you intend to do.'

'What do you mean?'

His eyes narrowed. 'Are you going to talk to your boss about accepting my new offer?'

Rose was still holding the piece of paper he'd given her and she carefully folded it and slipped it into her skirt pocket.

Returning her gaze to his, she said, 'I'll show him what you're offering—of course I will—but if you're asking if I'll try and persuade him to take it, then, no...I won't. Philip makes his own decisions—always has and always will. I neither have nor *want* any influence over him.'

'I don't believe you.' Dropping his hands to his hips, Gene smiled. 'I can sense that you're a sensitive woman,

Rose. I'm sure that Philip must appreciate that. If he knows that you care about his feelings then I'm sure he must respect any opinions you have about the matter and know that you have his best interests at heart.'

'Even so, it would feel wrong for me to persuade him to just sell the building, and some of the antiques, when he dearly wants to sell the business as a going concern.'

'But surely he must know by now that his beloved business clearly isn't viable any more?'

'Do you think I want to tell him that? When I know it's been his life's work and he's lying ill in hospital?'

'You would find a way to put it compassionately, I'm sure. You obviously care about him very much.'

'I do...'

'Then he is a lucky man.'

'*I'm* the lucky one. If he hadn't taken me on and taught me the trade I'd never have found the work that I've grown to love.'

'I'm sure he must have found it a pleasure to teach you, Rose. What sentient man *wouldn't*? Not only does he get a beautiful woman with captivating violet eyes and patrician cheekbones to work for him, but she becomes quite devoted to him too.'

Rose sensed her cheeks flush red. 'I think you've got the wrong end of the stick. Philip isn't attracted to me, if that's what you're implying, and neither am I to him. For goodness' sake—he's an elderly man, past retirement age!'

Gene was instantly apologetic. 'I'm sorry if I've caused offence. I thought he must be middle-aged, but

I didn't realise he was elderly. I'm afraid I confess I was a little jealous when I heard you talk about him in such glowing terms.'

Dry-mouthed, Rose hardly knew what to say. The way he'd complimented her looks just now was unbearably seductive, and saying that he'd been *jealous* of her admiration for Philip was crazy. Coming from a man who could have any woman he wanted, it was plainly ridiculous.

Realising that for a dangerous moment she'd been more flattered than she should, Rose gritted her teeth. Gene Bonnaire was even more of a threat than she'd thought...

'Look...I think you'd better just go. I mean it. I'll be in touch if I get any news from Mr Houghton for you.'

For a surreal moment Gene honestly forgot what he was about—because he suddenly found himself even more mesmerised by the brunette. Those violet eyes of hers were strangely bewitching, and he'd fallen into a bit of dream staring back at them.

He'd known when he kissed her that he wanted to seduce her...it was just a matter of *when*...but his sudden fierce attraction was honestly a revelation—because Rose Heathcote certainly wasn't the usual type of woman he was attracted to. She was not blonde, statuesque or shapely. She was small and slender, with black hair cut boyishly short. Yet the passionate spark in her eyes that he'd just witnessed, along with her feisty nature and her determination to protect her boss at all costs, made her surprisingly alluring.

It was another first, because Gene usually liked his

women to be more compliant. *He* liked to be the one in control.

Quickly returning to his senses, he realised he was just going to have to bide his time and wait for Rose to speak to her boss.

Moving across to the door, he glanced out at the now teeming rain and then back at the diminutive brunette. 'All right, then. I won't press you any further. But tell me… Is there anything I can do for *you*, Rose? Does someone as generous as you are, with your regard for others, ever have her kindness reciprocated? For instance I'd be *very* interested to know if you have a personal heartfelt desire. If you do, then all you have to do is say the word and I'll do my utmost to help you get it.'

'Why would you want to do that? I suspect it's because you have some devious ulterior motive…'

Gene laid his hand over his heart and grinned. 'You wound me deeply.'

'If you could give me my "heartfelt desire" then you'd be much more than a mere man. Has it never occurred to you that not all heartfelt desires are material ones?' Rose challenged him.

He shrugged. 'I can't say I spend much time thinking about it. I prefer to deal with the tangible, not the abstract.'

'So in your world feelings are abstract, are they?'

'Why don't you have dinner with me and we can talk about it?'

She grimaced. 'I'd rather have dinner with a boa constrictor! At least I'd know for sure what I'd be dealing with.'

In spite of his disappointment that Rose didn't seem to believe he might just want to give her something that pleased her, and at not immediately strengthening his chances to buy the property, Gene found her answer undeniably amusing. To his surprise, he also found it indisputably *seductive*...

'I can't say I'm flattered, Rose, but that's *funny*!'

'You should stop calling me Rose. It's Miss Heathcote to you.'

Gene smiled. 'I can see that I've really got to you, haven't I? All right, then—I'll go. But you haven't heard the last of me...not by a long chalk...*Rose*...'

He opened the door and, with a resigned grimace, walked out into the rain.

The phone rang in the early hours of the morning and a brisk-sounding nurse from the hospital informed Rose that Philip had taken a turn for the worse and asked if she could she please come in. Feeling numb with fear, she dragged on her jeans, T-shirt and Mackintosh and practically flew out the door.

When she got to the hospital and was directed to a ward she drew in a deep breath as she saw him. White-faced and fragile, he was lying in bed breathing through an oxygen mask and wired up to the kind of medical paraphernalia that told her this was serious.

All her worst fears crashed in on her at the same time. It hadn't escaped her notice that her boss had been transferred to the same ward that her father had been in when he died. He'd had a fatal coronary whilst in hospital for investigation into something relatively minor, so it had come as the most terrible shock. *Was this how Philip was destined to leave her as well?* Rose could hardly bear the thought.

The doctor on call had diagnosed pneumonia and he told her that it was crucial they stabilised the condition and that he got plenty of rest. To that end they would be keeping him in longer than they'd first envisaged, and would be treating him with antibiotics and extra oxygen.

As she sat by his bedside holding his hand, Philip opened his eyes just once, to acknowledge that he knew she was there, and she gently assured him that everything was going to be all right, that he wasn't to worry. But even as she said the words Rose didn't entirely believe them. Suddenly the man who had been such a firm friend to her and her father looked worryingly old and haggard…and very, very ill.

Having tried so hard to hold back the tears during her visit, as soon as she got home she threw herself onto the couch and the floodgates opened.

They weren't the last tears she cried over the testing week that followed. One day Philip was rallying encouragingly, looking a little better, and the next it seemed he was worse. Managing the shop as well as talking to an array of healthcare professionals about his aftercare, Rose was on a rollercoaster of emotion that one moment had her feeling hopeful for his full recovery and the next fearing the unthinkable…

She had all but forgotten her recent encounter with Gene Bonnaire. But one evening after work when she visited the hospital Philip told her he wanted to discuss something important. She had an uneasy feeling that the billionaire's offer to buy the antiques shop was on his mind. A couple of days earlier she had shown him Gene's offer. *She was right.* He clearly hadn't felt ready to discuss it then, but he did now.

'Rose…I want you to contact Mr Bonnaire and tell him that I'm going to agree to the sale.'

There was a flash of what looked to be deep regret in his pale blue eyes, and his expression was apologetic.

'I'm disappointed that he doesn't want to buy the business and that it won't continue as I'd hoped, but in my present situation beggars can't be choosers. Seeing as I haven't had any other offers, and I'm advised I'm going to be housebound for quite some time after this, I'll need to pay for private care. As you know, I don't have any family, but at least I have some material assets that I can realise to help me—the main one being the antiques shop. The man's offer for the building coupled with the antiques is more generous than I could have hoped for. He left me his card, didn't he? Can you contact him and arrange a meeting?'

Fighting to regain her composure at the idea that she was going to have to talk to the Frenchman again, Rose replied 'I'll do whatever you want me to do to help, Philip, but surely you can't meet with him to discuss things until you get out of hospital?'

Once more he was apologetic. 'I'm afraid I can't risk waiting that long. I need to sell the place as quickly as I can to free up some money for my care. I'm asking you to handle the sale for me, Rose. I've contacted my solicitor and he'll draw up the necessary papers. This is his name and number.'

He opened the bedside drawer, took out a single sheet of vellum that he'd written on and handed it to her.

'Anything you need to know, he'll explain.'

'It seems that you've made up your mind, then.' Frowning, Rose felt her muscles clench tight at the idea of once again coming face to face with Gene Bonnaire and knowing that this time *he* would be the one who had the advantage and would undoubtedly use it for all he was worth...

'Yes, my dear...I have.'

'Then I'll see to things right away. In the meantime you should try and rest as much as possible. The last thing you need is to be stressed about anything.'

Smiling fondly, Philip patted her hand as it lay on the counterpane. 'I should have told you this before, Rose... I don't know how I would have managed these past ten years without you. Without question, your loyalty, friendship and hard work have been invaluable and if I had been a much younger man I don't doubt I would have fallen a little bit in love with you.'

Feeling her cheeks glow warmly, Rose smiled back— even as she remembered Gene Bonnaire's ridiculous implication that her relationship with her boss might not be just a *working* one. *What she'd give to wipe that self-satisfied smirk off his handsome face when next she saw him!* Only she couldn't. She had to be nice to him because Philip urgently needed this sale. The last thing she would do was jeopardise things just because the man had rattled her.

But then, as she recalled that he'd asked her if other people ever reciprocated her kindness to them, she knew that the man had much more sensitivity than his very public persona suggested and thought that it would be intriguing to discover more...

'It's sweet of you to say so,' she answered Philip, 'but to be frank I think I'm destined to stay single. I've only been in love once in my life and it wasn't the happiest of experiences. I'm not eager to do it again.'

'I'm sorry to hear that. Don't you believe that it might be different the next time? Not so painful, I mean?'

'No, I don't. I don't because—present company not included—I don't trust men. I think I'd be better off on my own.' She shrugged. 'Besides, I'm far too independent, and men sense that. It would take someone pretty exceptional to get me to change my mind and I haven't yet met anyone who fits that particular bill.'

'Not yet, you haven't, Rose, but you will...you will.'

With a knowing smile, the man in the hospital bed closed his eyes and, leaving him to doze, she folded the sheet of notepaper he'd given her, slipped it into her bag and discreetly left...

CHAPTER THREE

STANDING IN ONE of his magnificent rooms, where huge plate-glass windows overlooked the ocean, Gene took the call from his secretary informing him that Rose Heathcote had requested a meeting. By the time he ended the call he was feeling more than vindicated. There could only be one reason why the feisty brunette wanted to see him, and that must be to convey the news that her boss had finally agreed to his offer.

He was elated. All his fantasies about owning the gracious building beside the Thames and turning it into the finest restaurant imaginable were becoming a dazzling reality in his mind.

He already knew the people he wanted to hire—both to do the renovations and to create and provide the cuisine that would be second to none. He had the private numbers of some of the finest chefs and sommeliers in the country, and he wasn't above using his money and power to entice them away from their current exclusive establishments. Before much time had passed the place would be up and running and he would be welcoming anybody who was anybody and yet again demonstrating to the world just how far drive and ambition could take a person if they were dedicated enough.

Make no mistake. Eugene Bonnaire was a force to be reckoned with.

His parents had never understood his ambition and drive for more…more money, more success, *more everything*… But they had both come from humble families in France, with barely a franc to keep body and soul together—hardworking folk who had barely eked out a sustainable living.

'Our families may not have always had enough food to put on the table but there was no lack of love in our homes,' his mother had often told him.

But the very idea of not having the most basic requirements had pained their son. No matter how much love they'd had, their lives had been pretty grim when they were growing up. Was it any wonder that Gene wanted so much more, to obliterate the stain of his ancestors' impoverished past?

Yes, his parents had made an admirable success of their East London restaurant, and their teaching him to cook at a young age had been a great platform for him to hone his culinary skills—a fact for which he was eternally grateful. It was that which had led to him becoming a much lauded chef, then a successful restaurateur. Add to that some eye-popping lucrative investments and the sky was his limit… But it had always been beyond him that his parents couldn't see that they could have had so much more for *themselves*…weren't even *interested*.

Breathing out a sigh, he rubbed his hand over his chest. It had been several months now since he'd paid them a visit and he knew they must be concerned. But he guessed that they didn't want to put pressure on him in case he did the unthinkable and cut them out of his life for good. *He would never do such a thing…* God knew they'd suffered enough.

When Gene had been just nine years old they had lost his little sister, Francesca, to a stomach virus. She had been only three. That shattering experience had changed them all. His mother had used to smile so easily—but not any more… There was always the sense that something vital and irreplaceable was missing when they were together, and of course there *was…*

Ever since that time Gene had sought to compensate his parents for their loss. If he became successful, he had reasoned, they would be so proud of him, and in turn he could ensure they enjoyed a comfortable old age. But somehow his success and ambition hadn't seemed to overly impress them. It was the one area in his life where he felt a failure. Consequently, his relationship with them had begun to deteriorate.

Feeling as though he'd lost the ability to properly connect with them, he had turned in on himself to protect his emotions. Inevitably, his other relationships had suffered. Women sensed that he wasn't available emotionally, and now the only women he seemed to attract were the ones who liked his wealth and what it could buy for them… That being the case, he'd decided to keep his liaisons short and sweet. More meaningful and longer-term relationships definitely weren't on his agenda…

But as he crossed the polished parquet floor to the door unbidden he suddenly found himself recalling the incandescent violet of Rose Heathcote's eyes. Without a doubt the woman intrigued and excited him. Gene mused that perhaps she wouldn't be so averse to his company now, when she would in effect be coming to him cap in hand because Philip Houghton had finally seen the sense in agreeing to sell him the shop. In any case, it meant that Gene would have the upper hand, and the diminutive Rose would no doubt have to swallow her pride and be nice to him.

He had no intention of making things easy for her either. Having not long ago arrived at his personal retreat on a remote Scottish island—the one place where he could genuinely enjoy some respite and didn't have to contend with petty jealousies and criticism from press and public alike—he wasn't about to charge back to London to sign the papers for purchase in a hurry. *Not when the tide had just turned in his favour.* No, he would insist that Rose brought them to *him*. Although he had never even invited family or friends to this house, he would make an exception for the brunette.

In that instant Gene knew that he would make it his mission to change Rose's mind about him. He would slowly reveal more of his true nature and let her see that, despite what she might have read and heard about him, he was at his core an *honourable* man.

As he opened the door and went out he felt more than a little pleased with his decision…

Faced with the prospect of spending time in a landscape as alien to her as the moon, Rose gritted her teeth and braced herself as a friendly Scottish boatman guided a sturdy fishing boat towards the island.

As fierce waves lashed at the sides and inevitably splashed her she couldn't help praying that she was doing the right thing in adhering to Philip's heartfelt plea to take the papers to the arrogant businessman and get the deal 'done and dusted' as quickly as possible. Philip had looked so poorly when she'd last seen him in the hospital that the need to arrange some full-time care for him when he went home—at least until he had recovered more fully—had become glaringly imperative.

'This is a rare event,' the young curly-headed boatman remarked cheerfully as he steered the craft towards a landing bay carved out between the rocks. 'As far as I know the Lord of the Manor never has women visit him here… In fact, he never has *anyone*. It's his private hideaway, he told me once. He likes the remoteness of the place. 'It helps him to think straight.' Grinning, he added, 'Must like you a lot, I'd say.'

Grimacing painfully, Rose answered. 'The truth is the man doesn't like me at all. The sooner my business with him is over and I'm heading away from here, the better.'

'Well, the soonest you can leave is tomorrow, lass. The tides dictate when you can come and go. They're a stern mistress to these remote islands.'

'I can't leave until *tomorrow*?' Crestfallen at the news, Rose wrinkled her smooth brow in distress. 'You mean I'll have to stay here overnight?'

'Yes, lass. I'm sure His Lordship will have made arrangements. Here we go—give me your hand and I'll help you out.'

Once on terra firma, although it was rocky and felt less than safe underfoot, Rose couldn't deny she was relieved to be on dry land again. The small craft had negotiated the choppiest of seas on their crossing and she couldn't attest to being remotely excited by it. Give her the ground beneath her feet any day. At least there she felt some small semblance of control.

Arranging the strap of her red leather tote more securely over her shoulder, she lifted her hand to shade her eyes from a watery sun and stared. The wind was groaning with a mournful howl and as far as she could see the surrounding landscape looked relentlessly bleak. She shivered hard.

There was no welcoming party in sight to greet her— but then she wasn't exactly surprised. Although Gene Bonnaire had arranged for a luxurious sedan to pick her up and take her to the airport, and had provided a business class ticket for her to travel on the plane, Rose wasn't resting on her laurels. The two encounters she'd had with the man had been both unpredictable and unsettling, but as she'd made the effort to travel all this way to bring him the documents to sign she thought he might at least have had the decency to meet her and take her up to the house.

'Likely he's forgotten what time you were arriving…' The boatman lifted a broad shoulder in an apologetic shrug.

'Can I get a signal here to ring him on my mobile?' she asked hopefully.

The boatman shook his head. 'Sorry, but we don't have any service. I'd take you up to the house myself, but I've got to make tracks straight away or lose the tide. See that path marked out up ahead? Follow it right to the top and you'll get to Four Winds. You can't exactly miss it. The house is like some huge glass fortress from a sci-fi movie.'

'What about the other people on the island? Where do *they* live?'

'They don't. Live here, I mean. When he's here, Mr Bonnaire is the sole inhabitant.'

Rose took a deep breath in. So, not only did she have to stay on the island tonight, but she would be marooned with one of the most unpredictable and challenging men she'd ever met. Now she really *did* have to grit her teeth.

As she turned to watch the boatman get back into his craft she had a real sense of being abandoned. She knew that wasn't good for her morale. The last thing she needed to feel when she came face to face with Gene Bonnaire again was unsure. The man had too many advantages as it was. And the most disturbing of all wasn't his power and wealth, but his arrogant belief that money could get him anything he wanted—that getting what he wanted was in fact his *right,* even if it meant remorselessly manipulating people to achieve it…

She addressed the young man who'd brought her over to the island. 'Will you be collecting me tomorrow?'

'Aye, it will be me. If you could be here in the morning round eleven I'll come and get you.'

'I wish it could be sooner…'

'You'll be all right, lass. His bark is worse than his bite.'

'You're a lot more confident about that than I am. By the way, I didn't ask your name or tell you mine. I'm Rose…Rose Heathcote.'

'You can call me Rory. It's nice to meet you, Rose. Well, I'd best be on my way. Take care, won't you? Chin up—and don't worry. Just look at His Lordship with those beguiling violet eyes of yours and he'll be putty in your hands! Bye, now!'

With a cheerful salute, Rory expertly steered the craft out of the rocky bay and headed out to sea.

Warmed by his jovial assurance, Rose stood for perhaps longer than she should have, watching the boat. It very quickly disappeared, engulfed by the wind and the rain and the thrashing waves as if it had never been. Offering up a silent prayer for the young boatman's safe journey home, she turned and negotiated some rocks that had been carved into paving stones and made her way onto the path marked out on the hillside.

By the time she'd made the deceptively steep climb to the end, even though on several occasions the icy wind had threatened to unbalance her and she'd had to watch carefully where she stepped, she was surprisingly warm, and she was more than a little out of breath when an impressive glass edifice loomed up before her.

Rory's description had been right on the money. Four Winds *was* like something out of a sci-fi movie. All that glass and chrome was a stunning contradiction, set in the bleak and yet beautiful landscape that embraced it.

Wiping away the sea spray that had moistened her face, Rose stared for what felt like an eternity, trying to make out where the entrance to the building was. Because it was a circular design, it wasn't easy to detect. There was no sign of Gene Bonnaire. How could she be sure he was even *there*?

As tense seconds turned into minutes she had a battle royal on her hands to keep her fury at bay. *What the hell did the man think he was playing at?* What if he'd changed his mind about his offer. What if he'd decided to pay her back for not agreeing to persuade Philip he should sell to him straight away and had made her come all the way out here to this remote Scottish island just because he *could*?

Her heart thumped so hard it felt as if it might burst out of her chest. If this was Gene Bonnaire's warped idea of a joke then it wasn't remotely funny...

'Well, well, well...look who the wind's blown in.'

The deeply gravelled tone almost made Rose jump out of her skin. Glancing up, she saw that part of the glass edifice had silently peeled back to reveal an entrance. Standing outside that futuristic doorway was the man she'd come to see. Dressed in fitted blue jeans that hugged his hard-muscled thighs and a black cashmere sweater, he had his arms casually folded across his impressive chest, giving the impression that it was the most natural thing in the world for him to come outside and find her standing there.

Clearly she wasn't going to receive an apology for his not meeting her off the boat...just his usual mockery. Her warmed hands had quickly turned icily cold while she'd been searching for the doorway, and now she gripped the strap of her tote hard as she fought to counter his cavalier treatment.

'You're lucky I'm here at all. I could have been blown off that hillside into the sea more than once on the way up here and you would have been none the wiser. Is this the way you usually treat your visitors?'

'No... It isn't...'

She had the briefest glimpse of what looked like regret in his fierce blue eyes—almost as if the idea had genuinely hurt him.

'I don't have any visitors here,' he stated. 'This is my private retreat and that's usually the way I like it. I've accorded *you* the privilege of coming here, Rose, because you have something that I very much want... and we both know what that is. However, I'm sincerely sorry that I wasn't down on the shore to meet you—I was busy with some work and simply forgot the time. I trust your journey wasn't too arduous?'

Rose suddenly felt ridiculously guilty. The Frenchman had sent a car to pick her up and take her to the station, and on the plane he'd arranged for her to travel first class. She had no complaints about the journey...

'It wasn't arduous at all. It's not every day that I get to travel business class. It was very pleasant, in fact.'

'Good. Well, you'd better come inside and get warm. And, by the way, there was no danger of you being blown off the hillside.' The corners of his eyes crinkled in amusement. 'You were too far inland for that.'

Biting back an irritable retort, Rose hurriedly moved

past him into a curved entrance hall. A sublime wave of welcoming heat enveloped her. Dropping her tote onto the pristine oak floor, she rubbed her hands together to restore their circulation.

Her reluctant host joined her and the chrome and glass wall behind him slid elegantly closed. She had a disturbing moment of fear, realising she didn't know how to open them again. Were the controls some kind of heat-sensitive mechanism that only recognised the house's owner?

Swallowing hard, she turned round to face him. 'The boatman—Rory—told me I'd have to stay here until tomorrow because of the tides. I don't want to inconvenience you, but I wish you'd told your secretary to tell me that before I travelled.'

'Would you still have come if I had?'

'Of course I would. I'm doing this purely to help Philip, Mr Bonnaire, so I'll do whatever is necessary.'

'Ah, Philip…' His tone suggested the idea that she should undertake what was clearly for her an unwelcome mission only because of loyalty to her boss irked him. 'How is he? Getting better, I hope?'

'As a matter of fact he's still in hospital. He took a turn for the worse. That's what has motivated him to accept your offer.' Rose's heart thumped a little harder as she was suddenly reminded of the precarious nature of her boss's health.

'I'm sorry to hear that. Please convey my wishes to him that he may get better soon. And, by the way, please call me Gene. Mr Bonnaire sounds ridiculously formal, considering the situation we're in. Why don't

you come with me into the sitting room and I'll get you
a hot drink?'

Rose wasn't so proud that she'd deny that was just
what she longed for. The chill on that hillside and in
the boat must have seeped into her bones.

'Thank you. I'd like that.'

Pushing her fingers through her short damp hair, she
retrieved her holdall and followed her host through what
seemed like an acreage of corridor into a wide, spacious
living area furnished with state-of-the-art minimalist
couches and chairs and a glass table long enough to seat
a small dinner party.

The vista through the huge uncovered windows was
breathtaking. The rain was pouring from the skies in
an endless stream now, and every time it lashed against
the flawless glass it was accompanied by the anguished
and ethereal sigh of the wind. But nothing detracted
from the stunning beauty that surrounded the futuristic building. The wildness of the sea and the terrain
were absolutely fitting.

Yet what was a successful entrepreneur who seemed
to have an insatiable desire for everything—be it property, land, not to mention beautiful women—doing with
a sanctuary in this wild, isolated place with just himself for company? Rose couldn't help feeling even more
intrigued.

'What would you like? Tea, coffee, hot chocolate?
Or perhaps you'd prefer something stronger?'

She swung her gaze round to meet Gene's. He looked
to be studying her with interest. His intense blue eyes
suggested he had the capacity to look right inside her,

and the idea made her shiver. The planes and angles of his face were uncommonly perfect, yet at the same time undoubtedly proclaimed him to be powerfully Alpha. He was so handsome that she couldn't help wondering what he would look like if he *really* smiled—if he was to drop that arrogant air of his for even a moment and genuinely connected with someone for no other reason than that it was *human*...

Shrugging off the notion because she sensed it was pointless, she replied, 'Hot chocolate sounds wonderful.'

'Your wish is my command. Why don't you sit down and make yourself comfortable? You can watch the storm that's coming, knowing you're sitting inside safe and warm.'

'There's a storm coming?'

'Of course...' He jerked his head towards the skyline. 'See those clouds that look like purple and black bruises? They definitely herald a storm. It's likely to be a big one, so all we can do is batten down the hatches and watch the entertainment. Are you up for watching nature at its wildest, Rose?'

She hadn't missed the provocative implication in his gravelled voice. Nor had she forgotten that scorching kiss he'd given her on his second visit to the shop. More than once the memory had made her catch her breath...

Arching a brow, she responded, 'None of us can control the weather—so why not? Seeing as my stay here was unforeseen, and isn't likely to be remotely pleasurable, it might be a welcome distraction and will help the time to pass more quickly.'

To Rose's astonishment he threw back his head and laughed. It was a full-throated, hearty sound that made her pulse skitter wildly and her blood heat. She'd told him that she didn't anticipate her stay would be pleasurable but in that unexpected moment, as the aloof businessman expressed a response to something that clearly elicited delight, once again she found herself helplessly warming to him.

'Can I ask what you find so funny?'

He dropped his hands to his straight lean hips and stared at her. 'I find your determination not to like me and your desire to leave my company as quickly as possible oddly endearing, Rose. I'm not exaggerating when I tell you that most women have the opposite reaction when they receive an invitation from me.'

'I'm sure it can't be just because of your scintillating personality…'

Gene's dazzling blue eyes narrowed. 'I agree, it's not my personality or even my looks that women are drawn to. Don't you think I *know* that? They're drawn to me because I'm a very rich man. I can buy them beautiful things and take them to all the best places. When they're with me it makes them feel special. It's not hard to work out why they like me. You're frowning. Does it surprise you that I would be so frank?'

Rose shivered as an icy drip of water slid off the ends of her hair and down onto the back of her neck, but her attention didn't waver for a second as she contemplated her host's chiselled countenance.

She sighed. 'More than finding it surprising, I'm disturbed that it doesn't bother you. I mean, can you honestly say that you're comfortable with women who only want to be with you for what you can give them materially?'

Right at that moment a flash of lightning still some way off on the horizon made her flinch, and thunder grumbled ominously. Although she'd deliberately made light of anticipating the 'entertainment' that was coming, thunder and lightning had always terrified her.

'I'm a realist, Rose. At least I don't kid myself. But you might also ask me if people disappoint me when they're so obviously shallow? My answer is *yes*…they do.'

They both fell silent for a while, each immersed in their unspoken reflections about the other…

It was Gene who ended the lull in the conversation. 'Before I get you that hot chocolate I'll show you into a guestroom and you can change out of those wet clothes. Do you have a spare set with you? If not, then I'm sure I can find you something.'

Surprised that he should be so considerate, Rose shrugged. 'Yes, I do. I brought a change of clothes with me in case I had to book into a hotel before I returned. It's a long journey to do in one day.'

'Good. Then follow me.'

As he guided Rose back out into the corridor and into the expansive area that housed the guestrooms— ironically for the guests he never invited—Gene knew a surprising pleasure at being able to help her to feel more comfortable. With her big violet eyes, her diminutive form and the dark hair that had been plastered to her head in the softly falling rain, she'd looked so small and delicate when he'd opened the door and found her standing there.

To his amazement, his pulse had inexplicably quickened at the sight of her. He'd never experienced such an unexpected reaction to a woman before and, disturbingly, he didn't think it was solely because she'd brought him the means to purchase the antiques shop building…

CHAPTER FOUR

RELIEVED TO FIND a hairdryer in the luxurious en-suite bathroom that accompanied the spacious guestroom, Rose sat on the capacious bed drying her damp hair. As the dryer blew welcome heat onto her scalp and neck she stared out through the surrounding bank of windows at the roiling sea and the ever more threatening darkening sky, her belly clenching at the thought of the storm that would very soon envelop them. She'd already witnessed one or two bolts of forked lightning in the distance and couldn't help flinching.

'Get a grip, Rose, for God's sake!' she scolded herself. But in truth it didn't help to engender confidence when she was going to have to sit out the coming elemental furore with Gene Bonnaire. As soon as he saw that she was scared would he mock her?

Recalling that he'd referred to the gathering storm clouds as being like 'purple and black bruises', she confessed to being surprised that he would use such a poetic turn of phrase. When he'd asserted that he had no interest in antiques whatsoever, Rose had wondered why they seemed to leave him cold. Couldn't he see the

beauty and artistry in their creation? It had bothered her
that he couldn't. Yet why refer to storm clouds as bruises
in the sky? Didn't that suggest there was something in
him that saw beyond the material? Some innate sense
that recognised the incomparable beauty and necessity
of nature, knowing that it was the one thing nobody had
any control over?

Rising to her feet, she returned the hairdryer to its
rightful place in the bathroom. As she turned she caught
sight of herself in the generous-sized gilt-edged mirror. Her skin looked white as alabaster and the dark
blue sheen in her black hair gleamed fiercely where it
caught the light. Most of all, her violet eyes looked big
and *scared*.

What was *wrong* with her? Was it just the coming
storm she was frightened of? Or was it the thought of
spending time with Gene?

Impatient with herself, she returned to the bedroom.
After hanging her Arran sweater in a mirrored ward-
robe whose doors swished open when she held her hand
briefly over an electronic button, as her host had demonstrated, she donned the fresh pink woollen one she'd
brought as a spare. Tugging it down over her jeans, she
pinched her cheeks to instil a little more colour into
them and then returned to the room that Gene had first
taken her to.

Rose was amazed when she found it easily. Clearly
her sense of direction hadn't let her down.

She found Gene seated on one of the futuristic
couches opposite the glass table, his elbows resting
against his hard-muscled thighs as he stared out of the

windows at the increasingly wild weather. Two steaming mugs were evident on the table as she approached.

Glancing up at her, he smiled. Startled, she fell headlong into his sublime azure gaze and forgot her own name. She'd never seen a man as beautiful... More than that, she had never experienced the forceful sense of a desire so profound that it stopped her in her tracks and—frighteningly—made it hard to breathe...

Gene's heart jolted and plunged him into a reverie of lust and longing that was unprecedented. Transfixed by the sight of the petite and pretty woman in front him, dressed in a girlish pink sweater and fitted blue jeans, all he could do was stare. What *was* it about her elfin features and ethereal eyes that made it hard to think straight when he looked at her? She wasn't a bit like any of the voluptuous women he was usually attracted to.

Suddenly aware that her appearance had rendered him momentarily dumb, he cleared his throat. Then he reached for one of the mugs of steaming hot chocolate and handed it to her. 'I see you found your way back, then? I've made your drink. You should sit down and enjoy it while it's hot.'

'Thanks. You timed it perfectly.' Accepting the proffered mug, Rose moved to the other end of the couch and sat down.

Gene's reaction at the distance she'd put between them was at first amused, then irritated. 'Why don't you come and sit closer to me? I promise I don't bite.'

Cupping her drink, she crumpled her smooth brow a little. 'That sounds like an invitation from the Big Bad Wolf...'

'Do you think of yourself as Little Red Riding Hood, then?'

'Why not? She was a very clever girl. She saw through the wolf right from the beginning. She knew he was up to no good.'

She flushed and Gene sensed his blood heatedly go south. How had he not seen just how engaging this woman was the moment he'd first set eyes on her?

Clearly unfazed by his teasing invitation to sit closer, she took an experimental sip of hot chocolate and licked her lips. The unknowingly provocative gesture had the effect of making his already entranced gaze hone in on the alluring shape of her mouth. The sight inevitably brought back the memory of the kiss he'd stolen at the antiques shop. He tightened as he remembered the luxuriant taste of her satin textured lips and the tide of molten longing that had flowed through him.

'My God, this is so good!' She smiled. 'How did you learn to make it so delicious?'

Once again Gene had to shake himself out of the trance he'd seemingly fallen into. 'My father taught me. He's a connoisseur in the art of making sinfully delicious hot chocolate. "Make this for the woman in your life, son, and she'll love you forever." That's what he used to say.'

'And do you? Make it for the woman in your life, I mean?'

He couldn't take the question lightly. Not when he'd never let a woman get close enough to engage his emotions, let alone make her his mate for life…

Disgruntled, he replied, 'No. I don't have a particular

woman in my life—and neither do I want to. I believe in keeping my options open.'

'You mean you'd prefer to have a selection of women to choose from rather than just one special one?'

He sensed an aggravated muscle jerk in the side of his cheek. 'I suppose you could say that.'

Rose's violet gaze was thoughtful. 'Then I guess I'm privileged that you chose to make hot chocolate for me, Mr Bonnaire, especially when I'm not remotely interested in joining your select little harem.'

'Indeed. And I asked you to call me Gene,' he snapped, unhappy that she should dismiss him so mockingly. It was hardly flattering.

Why on earth had he mentioned that silly comment his father had made? Not only had it highlighted to Rose that he liked to play the field—a fact he suddenly didn't feel proud of at all—but referencing the man who had raised him made him feel wretchedly guilty that he hadn't seen him in a while. It wasn't something he wanted to dwell on.

Pushing to his feet, he moved restlessly towards the panoramic windows and was momentarily captivated by the gigantic waves crashing violently against the rocks on the shoreline.

'Storm's getting wilder...' he murmured.

'Do they bother you...storms, I mean?'

Turning to smile at the woman Gene now realised was innately curious, he felt a frisson of excitement throb through him. What else might Rose be curious about if he were to delve a little deeper? he wondered.

'They don't bother me at all. I certainly don't fear

them, if that's what you're getting at. The more wild and furious they are the better, as far as I'm concerned. As you commented earlier, Rose, the unpredictable quality of nature is an ever-present reminder that people aren't in control of everything…even though some of us might like to think we are.'

His companion looked genuinely surprised. 'Forgive me, but I never guessed you could be so philosophical. You definitely gave me the impression that you're a man who likes to be firmly in control.'

For a long moment Gene contemplated the remark. Rose's deceptively calm demeanour gave no clue as to how feisty she was, or indeed how challenging she could be. Yet again he was taken aback that she dared to be so candid with her opinions. He wasn't used to that. It was true that he prided himself on being in control, but he didn't particularly enjoy it being pointed out to him. It might give his opposition an advantage. He also liked to steer the direction his conversations went in, so that they didn't stray into areas he didn't want them to go. He had a genuine fear of being exposed, of being seen as vulnerable in any way.

Biting back his irritation, he asked, 'And what about you, Rose? Do *you* like storms?'

As she set down her mug of hot chocolate on the table her expression was uneasy. 'Not particularly. To tell you the truth, they scare me. Not so much the wind and the rain, or even the thunder…it's the lightning I don't like. I've always been afraid of it. Once when I was little there was the most terrifying storm one night. Some lightning hit our greenhouse and shattered all the glass. It was like a bomb exploding. I was afraid to go back to sleep in case it happened again. No doubt that event has programmed me to be afraid of it for life. I have occasionally thought of getting some therapy...'

Finding himself intrigued, Gene moved back to the couch and sat down—but this time he deliberately positioned himself a little closer to Rose. 'It's not therapy you need, *ma chère*, but courage.'

'I'm not a coward.'

'Did I suggest that you were? Everyone has something they're afraid of. It's only human. No, what I'm saying is that you have to face your fears head-on. Expose them for what they are.'

'And what *are* they?'

Rose's voice had nervously dropped a little lower, and Gene saw the child she'd once been, too afraid to go back to sleep after lightning had shattered her greenhouse. It made him feel fiercely protective of her.

'They're just *illusions*. Thoughts in your head that don't serve you... Don't let them get the better of you or they'll dictate what you can and can't do for the rest of your life.'

'Is that how you handle *your* fears, Gene?'

For a sensually charged moment he absorbed the prickles of warmth that flared in his belly at the sound of his name on her lips, then he replied, 'Thankfully, they rarely arise for me—but, yes...that's how I handle them.'

'You mean there are no ifs or buts or maybes?'

'I don't let anything stop me from getting what I want, Rose—least of all *doubt*.'

'That's obviously why you appear to be so fearless, then?'

He didn't like it that she'd said *appear.* It suggested there was an element of doubt in her mind—that the confident image he projected wasn't all it seemed. Yet again Rose Heathcote was pushing all his hot buttons and the conversation was definitely taking a direction he didn't appreciate.

It seriously bothered him that he should be so unsettled by a woman, and he quickly sought to reassert his position.

'What you see with me is what you get, sweetheart. I don't need to resort to pretence. If you'd ever read my résumé you'd know that's a fact. My success speaks for itself. Now, as interesting as it undoubtedly is, I think we should bring this little conversation to an end. We'll both need something to eat soon, and I plan on cooking us dinner.'

Surprised, Rose quickly got to her feet. 'I don't want you to go to any trouble. A simple snack will do. I don't need a full-blown meal.'

'Say that to any top chef and they're likely to eject you from the restaurant. Food is more than just essential fuel, Rose… *Great* food is manna from heaven. A "simple snack" is not, and you won't be getting any such thing from me.'

Tucking her hair behind her ear, she felt her cheeks turn arrestingly pink. 'I meant no offence. But if you're insisting on cooking us a meal then the least I can do is help you…'

Gene immediately warmed to the idea. So much so,

he couldn't suppress a grin. 'So your talents go beyond being a devoted and able assistant in the antiques trade?'

She immediately looked stung. 'I'm not just an assistant. I'm a dealer in my own right.'

'Ah… That tells me that being valued and admired for your achievements *does* matter to you. We're not so different after all, are we? Very well, you can be my sous-chef tonight. Let's go into the kitchen and we'll get started.'

Gene handed Rose a white chef's apron and rolled up his sleeves. The tanned skin of his forearms looked silky smooth, and was dusted with a fine coating of dark hair.

As the rain thundered against the roof with increasing force, and the waves at the shoreline spewed icy foam against the jagged rocks, he instructed her on where she could locate the essential items they needed. The stunningly vast 'space age' kitchen didn't reveal its secrets easily. Drawers opened with the lightest touch, or a hand held in front of a discreet sensor, and the refrigerator and freezer looked as if they'd been designed by someone who excelled in writing sci-fi.

Rose's heart knocked anxiously against her ribs at being part of a scenario she would never have envisaged in a thousand years. From their first meeting Gene Bonnaire had challenged her. His too-confident air and superior manner unsettled her more than just a little. Add to that his reputation for acquiring anything he wanted simply because his money dictated that he could, in truth there was little to commend him to Rose.

She had never been the kind of woman who was easily impressed by a man, no matter what his credentials. A good character—someone honourable and loyal— that was what she secretly wanted in a man.

She'd once foolishly fallen for a stockbroker who had professed himself to be madly in love with her and wanted to marry her. But, although briefly dazzled by his declarations of adoration and devotion, Rose had soon found out that it was all a game to him. It had stroked his ego to think that she couldn't live without him. He'd enjoyed the power he had imagined it gave him over her. But his ambition to make money and go much further in his career had been his top priority— not *her*. And when she'd found out that she wasn't the *only* woman he professed to adore Rose had vowed never to make such a painful mistake again and had ended the relationship.

The man her mother had left her father for was also driven by money and status, and he was insufferably arrogant. Rose had not had cause to change her opinion in all the years she had known him. All she saw when she looked at David Carlisle was the man who had selfishly charmed her mother with his money and his looks just because it had stroked his ego to win over a happily married woman and—having won her—destroy her family.

When her mother, Ruth, had left it had been the first time Rose had seen her usually resolute father cry...

Gene Bonnaire was obviously cut from the same cloth as her ex *and* her mother's second husband, and she had plenty of reasons not to trust him. Hadn't he already indicated that he was an uncaring playboy—the kind of man who took what he wanted simply because his money and position allowed him to be as mercenary as he liked?

Yet here she was in his isolated sanctuary on a remote Scottish island, miles away from anywhere civilised, and until the boatman Rory met her tomorrow to take her back to the mainland she had to make the best of things. She'd sleep a whole lot better tonight if she didn't antagonise the man.

Despite all of that, she couldn't help recalling that crazily unreal moment when her gaze had locked with Gene's and molten desire had made her feel frighteningly weak. For a shocking instant there had been the urge to abandon all reason and surrender to the wild and wanton nature of it… How was any sane person able to explain such a thing?

Rose could only put it down to the fact that her guard was down after all the stress she'd endured recently. Philip was still in the hospital, and out of the blue he'd decided to sell the property to Gene.

One thing was certain: she would do everything in her power to make sure that a repetition of that crazy moment between them wouldn't happen. In fact she probably wouldn't rest easy until Gene had signed the documents she'd brought and deposited the funds for the sale into Philip's account. Then and only then would she be convinced that she'd done the right thing in coming here on behalf of the man who wasn't just her employer and mentor but her surrogate uncle as well.

Like many people who loved and appreciated craftsmanship in all its forms, after watching Gene effort-

lessly put the most sublime meal together Rose had to
attest that the man was a supreme artisan.

It had been fascinating to watch him work with his
hands. Whether it was slicing onions on a chopping
board, rubbing spices between his fingers and sprin-
kling them into the food as he stood over the stove, or
working the delicious ingredients he'd put together in
a pan with two or three economical stirs, she'd found
herself becoming more and more intrigued by the man.
With his handsome profile diligently focused, he looked
as if he inhabited another world when he was cooking,
and the so-called commonplace activity somehow made
him seem much more human…

'Should be ready soon—would you like a taste?'

In a near trance where she stood by Gene's side, Rose
glanced up at him in surprise. He scooped some food
from the aromatic pan onto a metal spoon and offered
it to her. *She didn't need to be asked twice.*

His compellingly blue eyes glinted knowingly as
she expressed her pleasure at what she'd tasted with an
appreciative groan.

'That's amazing! I've never tasted anything so delicious in my life…'

'Haven't you? That makes me want to give you more
delicious things to try.'

She felt her skin flame red, and a mixture of embar-
rassment and irritation throbbed through her.

But then Gene stepped towards her.

'You've got some sauce at the side of your mouth…
let me get it for you.'

With the pad of his thumb, he wiped it away. But it

was no simple gesture. The way he lingered over the task made it seem like some kind of erotic foreplay, and as he pressed his flesh against the side of Rose's lips it was as though he ignited a flame that wouldn't easily be extinguished.

There wasn't a single part of her body that didn't feel restless and hot. Trapped by his gaze, all she could do was stare helplessly. But at the same time her intuition alerted her to the danger... *What was she thinking?* Dear God, she was behaving as if she was *enjoying* his attention. One thing she was sure of: Gene Bonnaire didn't need another entranced woman pandering to his already inflated ego.

Stepping hastily away, she grabbed some kitchen towel and dabbed at her lips, unconsciously seeking to obliterate his touch.

Watching her, he released a low-voiced chuckle. 'I hope you're not feeling nervous around me, Rose? I told you I don't bite...' Levelling his chiselled jaw at her, he paused and smiled. 'That is unless you *want* me to?'

Rose's heart thundered so hard in her chest that she wondered he didn't hear it.

As adrenaline shot through her system on a dizzying white water rapid she straightened her shoulders and aimed for a withering glare. 'You know, you might think that *all* women enjoy your insincere flirtatious technique...that they should even be *grateful* for the attention...but I can assure you that *I* don't. That said, I think I should go and lay the table while you finish cooking the food.'

Opening a drawer that she'd learned was full of silver

cutlery she grabbed the necessary knives and forks and closed it again. Not waiting for further comment, she strode out of the kitchen with her head held deliberately high, praying as she went through the door that she'd remember where to locate the dining room...

CHAPTER FIVE

BRINGING A BOTTLE of Scotch whisky over to the coffee table, Gene poured some into the two waiting glass tumblers. His reluctant house guest was sitting with her shapely legs tucked beneath her on the couch, a satin cushion clutched to her belly, her transfixed gaze focused on the scene that played outside the windows as if she couldn't believe what she was seeing.

He'd witnessed a few wild storms since he'd built his sanctuary but never one quite like this. The thunder was akin to an earth-shattering sonic boom, whose power shook the walls of the futuristic dwelling he was so proud of. And the *rain*... The rain was like an enraged wild river that had burst its banks and was ruthlessly deluging everything in its wake. It was impossible to see where the sky ended and the ocean began.

And, like the most magnificent firework display ever conceived, the lightning had come.

They'd been expecting it for hours now, and had sensed the atmosphere growing thicker and thicker. It had grown so thick that *something* had to cut through it to lessen the tension.

Having arrived at last, the electrifying bolts that ripped through the atmosphere with their eerily bright light did exactly that. But the deafening noise and fury even made Eugene's heart jolt. Sensing a muscle tighten in the side of his jaw, he glanced at his companion. It was plain to see that she was more than a little jumpy.

'Rose?' Feeling an uncharacteristic sense of concern, he leant towards her and pressed a glass into her hand. 'I'd advise you to drink some of this. Not just because it's the best malt whisky in the world, and I only ever drink the best, but it might help calm your nerves.'

Although her hand shook a little, Rose tipped the glass back and gulped down some of the contents. Almost instantly her incandescent violet eyes flooded with tears. Then she started to cough.

Gene reached round to pat her on the back, his lips shaping an amused smile. 'You drank that down a bit too quickly, sweetheart. Make the next sip a little slower, hmm…?'

Returning his wry look, she commented, 'I'll bear that in mind. It's pretty powerful stuff, isn't it?'

'This particular blend is smoky, sweet and smooth. But I don't doubt to a novice it can still pack a punch.'

Even as he was speaking a fierce display of dazzling lightning lit up the room, highlighting everything in full cinematic glory.

'Oh my God!' Visibly shocked, Rose all but threw herself against him.

Even though he knew it was purely a reflex reaction, instigated by fear, Gene was inordinately pleased that in that instant she genuinely seemed to need him. He'd never experienced anything remotely like the feeling before, and it made his heart race a little.

As the gentle scent of her summery perfume made provocative inroads into his senses he draped his hard-muscled arm round her slender shoulders and pulled her a little closer to him.

His beard-roughened jaw glanced against the silkily soft strands of her ebony hair and he murmured, 'It's all right, Rose. Nothing's going to hurt you…I promise…'

At first she stiffened at the assurance, and then she relaxed.

Relieved, Gene was glad she didn't pull away. Despite the storm raging outside, he felt strangely peaceful as he sat there with Rose. He had a distinct sense of being introduced to an aspect of his character that he'd never before suspected. The only woman he'd ever felt remotely protective towards before was his mother. His more intimate female relationships all centred round money and sex. *His* desire for sex and *their* desire for money… Genuine intimacy didn't feature. How could it when he'd allowed himself to become more and more distant from his feelings? Since his little sister had died the spectre of loss and heartbreak was ever-present, and in truth he *feared* it…

The soft weight against his arm grew a little heavier and Rose's quiet, steady breathing made Gene realise that she'd fallen asleep.

It seemed to be a day of shocks and surprises, he thought wryly. Not only had the ferocity of the storm taken him aback, but the realisation that he wasn't just *enduring* his visitor's company but was actively *enjoy-*

ing it really rattled him. His pleasure at being able to purchase the lovely old shop building hadn't dominated his thoughts half as much as he'd expected it to.

He frowned. *Why was that?*

Settling back more comfortably against the cushions, hardly aware that he was doing so, he drowsily let his eyelids drift closed…

The first thing that alerted him to the realisation that he'd fallen asleep was Rose trying to disengage his arm from her shoulders. Eugene cursed…*loudly.* The limb had cramped painfully, and in the throes of sleep he thought someone was attacking him. His primal masculine instinct was automatic.

When he sat up and grabbed his imagined attacker Rose yelped, and the shocked look on her face woke him up to the reality of what he was doing. His hands were tightly gripping her arms through her soft woollen sweater and she looked absolutely terrified. Albeit indignant…

Even as he lessened the pressure of his fingers on her arm he was suddenly mesmerised by the inviting shape of her luscious mouth. Her beautiful eyes were shining like stars. Staring back into that hypnotic violet glance was like falling into another dream…one that he was in no hurry to wake up from.

'Let go of me,' Rose breathed huskily.

Gene heard the words, but even as he registered them he was helplessly bending his head towards her. His body was heavy with desire, and only the taste of those lush tender lips would alleviate some of the insatiable erotic need he was suddenly inflamed by.

'Not yet…' he whispered, and claimed the mouth that unknowingly taunted him as if it were a choice between breathing to live and *not* breathing.

If he'd had any expectations that first time he'd kissed her, then the touch of Rose's lips beneath his had exceeded them all. Now, for the second time, the sensation was beyond wonderful. And the most pleasurable surprise came when she gasped softly, didn't resist his urgently seeking tongue as he thought she might, but instead welcomed the heated exploration as if she needed it as much as he did.

The hot satin interior of her mouth sent his temperature skyrocketing, and Gene's fingers moved through her silky hair to anchor her head and explore her flavours more deeply. Again, Rose showed no sign of protesting. His heart was galloping hard and the strangest feeling washed over him. It was an inexplicable sense that he was diving too deep ever to surface again without some serious damage having been caused…

Rose could hardly believe she was passionately kissing Gene Bonnaire. Had she unknowingly suffered some kind of bump to the head and been transported to an uncanny parallel universe where everything she'd known to be real had vanished? Who could blame her for that conclusion when the violent storm outside was growing ever more ferocious, adding to the sense that she was in some kind of twilight world? Being marooned in this isolated dwelling with a man she'd undoubtedly give a wide berth to if she met him under any other circumstances just didn't make sense. *Yet perhaps it wasn't as unbelievable as it seemed.* How

could she have known that this avaricious businessman could seduce her with his unexpected displays of
care and concern?

First he'd dispensed advice on dealing with her fears.
Then he'd cooked a sublime French dish that had been
nothing less than exquisite. And finally...*finally* he'd
put his arm around her and held her against him when
the lightning had looked to be heralding the end of the
world and she'd been terrified.

Was that why she'd found herself willingly kissing
him...? Because she was grateful for his protection?
Had the feeling awakened some latent desire she'd been
burying?

Her father had always sought to protect her from
harm and keep her safe, and she'd trusted him more
than any other man. Was she hoping to find someone
similar in her romantic life? But Gene Bonnaire was
nothing like her father had been. The billionaire was
known to be utterly ruthless in pursuing his desires, and
he had a reputation for letting nothing stand in his way.
Yet when he'd held her against his powerful chest as
they'd watched the storm Rose had trusted him enough
to fall asleep.

How to explain it? All she knew was that she hadn't
been able to resist him. Everything about the man
seemed to dazzle her...the way he looked, the way he
smelled, his sheer indomitable maleness... The realisation confused her. It also made her wary about the
danger she might be inviting. She only had to remember her ex and the way he'd blatantly lied to her to get

what he wanted... Gene was another man who liked the sense of power money could give him...

When Gene carefully separated his lips from hers, his long fingers stroking her hair back, he smiled down at her with a knowing glint in his piercing blue eyes and she knew it was time to end this craziness and return to some kind of normality.

When she explained to him why she'd succumbed to that kiss—she'd been stressed and worried about her boss, and scared of the lightning—hopefully he would understand and not use the minor aberration against her.

Flattening her hand against his chest, she started to move away.

Frowning, Gene reached out to pull her back. 'Where are you going?'

For a moment Rose couldn't think what to say, because his glittering blue eyes were holding her to him as securely as if they'd been bound together.

'I shouldn't have done that. I'm sorry.'

'Why? Didn't you enjoy it?'

'That's not the point. The point is I'm here solely on business. And you're not responsible for comforting me just because I'm scared of lightning.'

'Would your boyfriend have comforted you if he'd been here?'

'What's that got to do with anything?'

His eyes narrowed. '*Would* he?'

'I don't have one.' Rose lifted a shoulder in a shrug, her gaze unflinching. 'I'm not interested in having a relationship at the moment.'

'Presumably that's because you're concerned about your boss?'

'It's not just that. I want to concentrate on my career. When Philip leaves the antiques shop, so will I. I'll have to find another position.'

'Presumably that won't be difficult? You're a qualified dealer, you said.'

She lifted her chin, as if to challenge him to doubt her. 'I am. And if I can't find anything suitable back home I might go abroad for a while and work.'

It was definitely an option, but somehow she didn't feel quite ready to take such a bold leap. She'd like to think she could make things work at home first. Anyway, the thought reminded her of what was most pertinent now.

Meeting the diamond-bright glance that had barely left her since they'd kissed, she said, 'Getting back to the reason I'm here... Don't you think we'd better deal with the signing of the documents tonight rather than leave it until the morning? It's just that I want to make sure I'm ready in plenty of time to meet the boat. The sooner I get back to the hospital and see how Philip is doing, the better.'

'I won't be signing anything until I'm satisfied that everything is in order. Give me the papers and I'll look over them tonight. Then we'll see what the morning brings.'

Dry-mouthed, Rose stood up. Gene's enigmatic comment had left her feeling as though she'd just plunged down a flight of hard-edged stone steps. 'Are you suggesting that there might be a possibility you *won't* sign?'

As he got to his feet his expression was tight-lipped and serious. 'Make no mistake. I want the property. That desire hasn't changed. But it's a policy of mine never to sign anything until I'm sure.'

'You mean you got me to come all the way out here in the *belief* that you were going to buy, but now you're not *sure*? Is this some kind of warped game you're playing?' She shook her head in despair. 'I should have known as soon as I saw you that you weren't to be trusted, but it seems I never learn…'

He moved closer. So close that Rose could see the gentle indentations in his otherwise smooth skin where the dark stubble of his beard had started to grow. His warm breath drifted over her face and made her teeth clench.

'What do you mean by that? Has someone let you down, Rose? Was it an ex-boyfriend, perhaps? If that's true, then I'm sorry. But this isn't a game I'm playing… it's the way I do business. I set out my intentions, believe without a doubt that what I want is going to be mine, and then I take some time to enjoy the realisation before I finally take the prize.'

She swallowed hard as he reached out and laid his palm against her cheek. It was clear that he wasn't just referring to his purchase of the antiques shop building.

Rose felt alternately hot and cold. Did he think that she'd fall into bed with him because she'd so willingly returned his kiss? He'd caught her off guard—that was all.

It was her cue to firmly lift his hand away and engineer some distance between them. Folding her arms over her sweater, she glanced out at the scene before her. Although the storm was still evident, somehow it seemed less ferocious. Sounding more like a subdued grizzly bear now, rather than a rampaging tiger, the thunder continued to rumble but the lightning was definitely lessening. Electrical flashes of cobalt pierced the sky here and there, but they were starting to suggest a once rampaging force now spent and retreating, and she was more than a little relieved.

However, Rose was still anxious that she might not be going home with the business sold and the funds deposited into Philip's bank account after all. A sleepless night was definitely on the horizon, because it wasn't going to be easy to wait until the morning for Gene's decision.

She was quickly learning that the man was a bit of a wild card...a law unto himself. That was a challenge. If for any reason he should change his mind about buying, what could she do but walk away in defeat? The situation might grieve her, but she hardly had the power to make him reconsider, did she? And he didn't look to be the type of man who would be swayed by any sense of compassion.

Rose was dreading taking such demoralising news back to Philip. What if it caused his health to deteriorate even more? The only thing she could do now was stay as calm as possible and not let her host see how perturbed she was.

'Well, there's not much more to say, then, is there? I'll go and get the purchase documents and give them to you to look over.' Glancing down at the pretty platinum wristwatch her father had given her for her twenty-first birthday, she added, 'After that I think I'll say goodnight.'

Turning towards the door, she was stopped in her tracks by Gene's intimate gravel-voiced reply.

'If we have any more lightning during the night and you're feeling scared my room is just down the hall from yours. I'm a very light sleeper, so don't hesitate to knock and come in, will you?'

Clenching her fists down by her sides, Rose prayed for the strength not to succumb to the pure unadulterated temptation the hard-chiselled specimen of masculinity before her exuded with a mere glance...let alone the sexy bass voice that reeled her in like a fish on a hook...

'I'm sure I'll be fine,' she said airily. 'I'll simply use that technique you told me about and remember that my fears are just illusions.'

She swore she heard Gene chuckle in amusement as she walked to the door and went out...

He had another restless night. It wasn't so easy to fall asleep when he knew that Rose slept just a short walk away from him, down the corridor in one of his guest-rooms. Somehow Gene couldn't shake the memory of that inflammatory kiss he'd stolen from her. All night it tempted and mocked him, until the fervent hope of a repeat performance finally lured him into sleep with its promise. But then he dreamt of holding Rose in his arms and making passionate love to her, and he woke at sunrise with his body coated in perspiration and heavy with desire.

Why hadn't she come to him in the night as he'd hoped? The storm had returned round three a.m. and the lightning had once again been spectacular. Surely she couldn't have slept through such a display? Had stubborn pride stopped her from seeking his reassurance?

Even though he admired her tenacity, he had to find out for himself how she'd fared. Quickly showering and dressing, he glanced at the property sale documents he'd examined minutely into the early hours and took them with him into the living room. There was no sign that his guest had been there.

His stomach clenching with nervous excitement at the thought of seeing her, he left the papers he'd been studying on the coffee table then returned to the room he'd allocated to Rose. He rapped sharply on the door. She didn't answer straight away and Gene was immediately concerned.

He was about to knock again when the door opened. 'Morning…' she murmured. Paler than usual, and distinctly bleary-eyed, her appearance suggested that she too had had trouble sleeping. Her black hair was prettily tousled but her skin looked as smooth and delicious as a peach. She was still in her nightwear—a short white satin affair, with spaghetti straps—and one of the straps had drifted down over a slim shoulder.

Gene took a moment to assemble his emotions. Once again he felt concerned and protective. It was so unlike his usual response at seeing a woman he desired that it honestly perturbed him.

'Good morning,' he greeted her. 'Don't tell me you didn't see and hear the lightning last night because I won't believe you.'

Groaning, she was already shaking her head and tunnelling her fingers through her hair. 'I'm not going to lie. I didn't sleep a wink. I wouldn't say no to some coffee if you're making it?'

'Never mind the coffee—why didn't you knock on my door like I told you to?'

Even as he asked the question Gene stepped over the door's threshold and, with no intention other than to reassure her, wound his arms round her impossibly slim waist. The act was his undoing. The combination of the silky satin nightdress and the warm, shapely body beneath his hands aroused him more than he'd ever been aroused before…to the point where he couldn't help but act on sheer primal instinct.

'I would have held you close all night…protected you…' he murmured.

In between each word of the huskily voiced affirmation he touched his lips to Rose's hair then, hearing her gasp softly, he tipped up her chin and touched them to her mouth. The irresistible fusion was hot, sultry…and almost beyond controllable…

Rose glanced up into his eyes, the flat of her hand resting lightly against his chest. But this time there was no suggestion that she wanted him to leave.

'I—I can't seem to think straight when I'm around you,' she confessed. 'I didn't come to you last night because I was afraid of what might happen.'

'What did you think might happen?'

'I feel like—like I'm under some kind of spell when I'm near you and that makes you dangerous.'

'You think *I'm* the one who's dangerous? You're the one that's cast a spell, you little witch…'

'You should go,' she breathed, but her fingers were curling into his shirtfront and her eyes were full of longing.

Gene needed no further invitation. 'Sweetheart, I don't think so…' he murmured.

Sweeping her up into his arms, without further ado he carried her across to the lavish double bed. As he laid her down against the rumpled silk sheets his heart beat so fast he was dizzy. Rose wasn't looking sleepy any more. She looked wide awake, her flawless complexion no longer pale, but softly rouged pink with desire…

As he started to lower the spaghetti straps of her nightgown down over her shoulders, so that the satin mounds of her breasts were more evident, he couldn't resist a grin. 'If I'd known you wore such sexy nightwear I would have battered down your door and come to you last night. Honest to God, I would have,' he swore.

For answer, she made a helpless little sound of hunger and pulled his head down to hers. As they kissed Gene reached down to his back pocket and drew out the foil packet he kept there. There were no more words after that. There was no need. His whole world had narrowed down to these few heatedly charged moments, to the beautiful woman beneath him and their hungry, *insatiable* need for each other.

When he finally took her, with Rose's strong, slender thighs wrapped round his middle, he honestly thought he'd died and gone to heaven. It wasn't just her kisses and her body that were heavenly—everything about her was divine. Already he knew there was no way on earth he would be satisfied with just taking his pleasure and then setting her aside, as he usually did with the women in his life. A strong desire to *really* get to know her was building inside him.

As she quickly came to her fulfilment her thighs clamped him even tighter and she rode the wild waves that took her. Staring back into her superlative violet gaze, Gene soon followed, issuing a harsh-sounding cry that seemed to emanate from deep inside him. In the aftermath of his climax he was rendered both breathless and speechless for a while before he came back to himself. Then he lay down next to Rose and gently pulled her into his arms.

'*Tu es incroyable*...' he whispered into her ear.

Her pretty cheeks dimpled. 'I like it when you speak French. You can whisper some more to me, if you like?'

'Right now I'd willingly do anything you wanted, *ma chère.*'

'I might hold you to that...' With a teasing but knowing smile, Rose held her hand softly against his cheek...

CHAPTER SIX

ROSE HAD IMMEDIATELY sensed the man beside her tense when she'd asserted that she would hold him to his comment about doing anything she wanted. She hadn't meant anything by it—it had just been a bit of teasing banter. But now, up and dressed, she felt her own tension mounting as she followed him out into the living room.

She could hardly believe what had just happened between them. All she knew was that making love with Gene had made her feel more alive and vital than she'd felt in years... However, as wonderful and exhilarating as the experience had been, she'd better quickly come back down to earth and remember why she was there.

With his straight back and squared shoulders—his flawless white shirt and taupe chinos a little crumpled after his joining her in bed—Gene looked intimidating and officious. That suggested he wasn't going to be as approachable as he recently had been. Obviously he had reached a decision about the antiques store, and perhaps it wasn't the one she'd hoped for...

Would he let her down gently or would he stress that business was business and he no longer saw the building as a viable proposition for his restaurant business? Suddenly Rose was sick with nerves. How would she tell Philip about her failure to bring back the signed purchase agreement if that was the case?

She could already visualise the pain and disappointment in his eyes, even though she knew he would quickly reassure her that everything would be okay— that he would soon find another buyer and all would be well.

Her mind teeming with thoughts, most of them unhelpful, all of a sudden Rose was struck by how bare and austere the white-painted room was. Yes, it had a magnificent view, but how much more beautiful it would look if it had some warmth and personality instilled.

'What a shame you don't like antiques or even beautiful paintings,' she declared. 'The right ones would make this room look even more stunning…it would be so much more homely and inviting.'

Gene turned round. Raising a formidable dark brow, he snapped, 'But this isn't my home. It's my retreat. I don't need pictures or antiques to pretty it up. Besides, no one else is going to see it but me.'

After the intimacy they'd just shared, Rose was more than a little deflated by his sharpness. But she persisted. 'That might be the case, but what's wrong with *you* appreciating them? Surely you would find some pleasure in making your retreat look nice on the inside as well as externally?'

'You're wrong. I wouldn't. It serves a purpose—
that's all it does. I'm not interested in getting any pleasure from what the furnishings look like.'

His tone was adamant…not to mention he seemed
annoyed that she'd made the suggestion.

'I'm not an aesthetic like you are, Rose. I'm practical and pragmatic.'

'Yet it's important to you to wear beautifully tailored
clothing, shoes made by one of the finest Italian designers and the most appealing French cologne, isn't it?'

As soon as the words were out of her mouth Rose
sensed her blood throb heatedly through her veins. So
hot and heavy did it pound that she was mortified. She'd
revealed to Gene that she'd noticed so much. In doing
so, she'd foolishly given him another edge with which
to usurp her if he chose and, despite their lovemaking,
she didn't doubt that he would use it…

She saw that his deliciously carved mouth had shaped
a smile. Again the image of the Big Bad Wolf flashed
into her mind.

'You're right. I admit that personal presentation is
important to me. And to that end I believe in wearing
only the very best that money can buy.' He paused, and
a muscle flexed at the side of one flawlessly carved
cheekbone. 'It goes without saying that my exacting
standards are important in my personal life too. For
example, I very much appreciate the curves of a lovely
woman…the way she smiles…the radiance of a pair of
stunning long-lashed violet eyes…'

He was talking about *her*. Rose sucked in a steady-
ing breath as her heart beat double-time. The irresist-

ible magnetism between them which had driven them to consummate their attraction wouldn't have been there under normal circumstances, she was sure. It had probably just occurred because they'd found themselves isolated and alone in this incredible futuristic house, with nothing but the rocks, the sea and the stormy weather to keep them company. Add to that Rose's fear of lightning, and the fact that she'd let her guard down round Gene because he seemed so concerned...

A disquieting thought assailed her. What if his being concerned was just an act and in truth he just wanted to have her in his power because it stroked his ego? After all, he prided himself on having anything he wanted, didn't he? But she still couldn't understand why he didn't seem able to resist her. It just didn't make sense. *Nothing* made sense when she was around him, she realised.

Clasping her hands in front of her soft woollen sweater, she didn't shy away from meeting his gaze. She had come here for one thing and one thing only: for him to sign the documents that would make him the new owner of Philip's antiques store. That was what she should be concentrating on.

'Well, that aside... Have you made a decision about the antiques shop?'

He gave her another enigmatic smile. Yet the charismatic gesture on that too handsome face hardly reassured her. It did, however, make her catch her breath. And the restless heat that seemed to have infiltrated her body because she now knew what it felt like to be intimate with him seemed to increase disturbingly.

His comments just now suggested that he thought her beautiful, and the exhilarating thought affected Rose perhaps more than it ought to. The allure of him was becoming more and more irresistible, and along with the impulse to do what was right and be sensible it had created a war inside her that made it hard to think straight.

Her voice not quite steady, she pressed, 'Well? You need to tell me sooner rather than later, because I have a boat to catch.'

'Do you?'

He was moving closer still, and the faint drift of his arresting French cologne made her stomach clench painfully. 'What do you mean do I? How else am I going to get off this island and return home?'

'I meant does it have to be today?'

Rose widened her eyes. 'Why? Is there some reason I *shouldn't* go today?'

Gene was suddenly standing right in front of her, and his crystalline blue gaze was hot enough to burn her. 'Yes, there is. I'd like you to stay so that we can get to know each other a little better.'

There was a dizzying rush inside her head. 'Why on earth do you think that—?'

Before she could finish what she'd been going to say her lips were captured hungrily, and suddenly there was no oxygen left to breathe—just a heady, seductive heat and the taste of something forbidden...

With a helpless groan Rose found herself responding. The thought *how can something so wrong seem so right?* flashed through her mind. Sexually, the man delivered everything he promised. She found herself strangely weak, with a hard to resist desire to be more reckless than she'd ever been before…

Last night she'd been terrified by the violent flashes outside the window that had lit up her room like every celebratory firework display in the country combined. Yet she'd been more afraid of knocking on Gene's door to let him know because of what might happen if she did. But then in the morning…*it had happened anyway.*

His hands were on her shoulders now, and they moved seductively down her back, the scalding heat from his fingertips feeling as if they were melting the very vertebrae of her spine as they travelled. Then he caught her by the waist and impelled her closer—so close that she was intimately aware of his heat and his hardness again.

He felt so good…so…so *necessary.* The man's kisses were an erotic delight that she could easily become addicted to.

He was still kissing her when he reached for the hem of her sweater and started to tug it upwards. When he lifted it over her head and let it fall onto the floor behind her Rose's heart galloped. She was wearing a sleeveless white vest over a matching cotton bra, and when Gene's searching hand dived inside to caress her breast, his fingertips lightly pinching her burgeoning nipple, she moaned feverishly. Then he carried on kissing her—as if he too was finding it hard to be free of the taste of her.

It felt so good to be wanted and desired. It had been a long time.

Her last and only real boyfriend, Joe Harding, had been a twenty-four-year-old trainee broker, and at the age of eighteen she had lost her virginity to him. At first he had been kind and considerate, swearing that he loved her. But as time progressed he'd become more and more driven by the demands of the City bank where he worked and hadn't seemed to have much time for anything else—including their relationship.

He'd sought to placate her by telling her that he was working hard for *her*...that he wanted to ensure that they had a happy and successful future *together*. But Rose had soon begun to suspect that that wasn't true. One night she had smelled another woman's perfume on his shirt and, when confronted, he had admitted that he'd been having an affair...as it turned out one of many.

She had been horrified and hurt that the man she'd so eagerly given her trust and her love had so blatantly betrayed her. She'd had a short, sharp lesson in the mercenary way some men could behave...and in the lies they told to get what they wanted, not caring who they hurt in the process. Heartbroken, Rose had told him it was over. He hadn't even looked surprised, and nor had he protested. *In fact, she'd never forgotten the look of relief in his eyes...*

After that wounding experience she'd vowed to stay single and focus on her career, and she hadn't succumbed to any soulless liaisons purely for physical release either—no matter how tempted she sometimes felt—knowing it was only because she was lonely.

Yet here she was, in the arms of a man who was the ultimate practised seducer, and she would have utterly surrendered to him for a second time if he hadn't lifted his head right then to examine her with what looked like a knowing smile. If ever a man epitomised the 'cat that had got the cream', *he* did.

Her insides plunged and a deafening alarm bell rang inside her. Rose was suddenly painfully reminded of exactly who Gene Bonnaire was. He was a mercenary businessman who didn't have a single qualm about taking what he wanted—and he was just about to add her body and her capitulation to his self-aggrandising quota of conquests if she didn't take action and stop him.

Breathing heavily, she pushed his hands away and stumbled as she stepped back to collect her discarded sweater. She was still reeling from that too knowing smile. Hurriedly pulling on the garment, she wiped the back of her hand across her throbbing lips in a gesture of disgust.

Startled and disappointed, Gene shook his head.

Rory's boat couldn't arrive soon enough, as far as Rose was concerned. The sooner she was out of there and away from this man the better. However, there was still the important matter of the shop to address.

'You didn't answer my question. Do you still intend to buy the antiques store? If the answer is yes then you'd better get on with signing the papers so I can get ready to leave for the mainland.'

She was still breathing hard as she spoke, unsure of how she would handle Gene's reaction. The feeling brought it home to her how little she knew him. Did anyone *really* know this man who had built a sanctuary for himself on a remote Scottish island?

'Why did you break off our embrace? And don't lie to me and tell me you weren't enjoying it. Or do you get some kind of perverse pleasure from leading a man on?' he demanded.

'I didn't lead you on. I've already let myself down by going to bed with you. I freed myself just now because it suddenly hit me what I was doing. You have a reputation for unscrupulously taking the things you want without giving a damn about the consequences— and I didn't come here to end up as another one of your forgettable conquests. Even though you might call me a hypocrite because of the way I've acted around you, thankfully I've come to my senses. So let's forget what just happened and get on with our business, shall we?'

Stealing a quick glance at the time on her watch, Rose swallowed hard. Although she was adamant she would stay strong, inside she was quaking.

'I've got exactly one hour before I have to be down on the shore to wait for the boat.'

Gene stood perfectly still. As he examined her, his expression was bleak. 'Well, Rose… It seems as if I've misjudged you. I thought you were different from all those people who so avidly believe everything they read in the papers about me…about my less than flattering "reputation"…but I see that I was wrong.'

All of a sudden she felt sickeningly faint. *Was* she the one who was guilty of misjudging?

The usually arresting gleam in his eyes was gone. The burnished light was dulled.

'Did you honestly doubt that I would sign the purchase papers? There was never any chance of that. I still plan to own the property. It's just that I'd hoped I might persuade you to spend some time with me and not hurry to return.'

Rose was in turmoil. Should she believe the desire he'd expressed to spend more time with her was because he genuinely wanted to get to know her, or because he simply saw an opportunity to engage in another sexual liaison? It was so hard to trust Gene when all she had to go on was her bitter past experience of being let down by a man who had put his ambition and desire for money before his desire to have a loving relationship...

Gene smiled—but the blue eyes were chillingly empty now, she saw. He looked as though he expected her just to wait for him to sign the papers and then walk away...

'I can see that you plainly don't want to do that. You'd better follow me into my office.'

He strode ahead of her through the door, the heels of his black Italian loafers echoing loudly against the parquet flooring. Rose had to practically run to keep up with him.

Dropping down into the sumptuous leather seat behind the elongated glass desk that occupied another vast and mostly empty white room, Gene calmly drew the sheaf of property documents towards him. Silently scanning the opening page, he reached for the glinting gold fountain pen on his blotter.

Lifting his gaze, he looked straight at Rose. 'You may as well sit down,' he told her.

Still shaken after hearing his confession that he'd hoped she might stay a little longer, she sat down in the elegant leather chair on the opposite side of the desk. She could still feel the sensation of his hot velvet mouth against hers…still taste him…and she wanted to cry— because after she'd left this remote and isolated place she would never experience such delights again.

'There's one small proviso before I sign,' he declared.

Rose's heart stalled. 'What's that?'

'I want your agreement that you'll help offload the antiques for me. I'll pay you for doing it. I've already told you *I* haven't any use for them, but that doesn't mean I want to *give* them away. I can see that some of them are valuable, and that's reflected in the price I've paid for them. You know the market, and I sense you won't let them go for a song. So, do I have your agreement, Rose?'

How could she possibly say no when Philip needed every penny to help towards his aftercare when he returned home? It shouldn't be such a dilemma, Rose thought, but because it would mean she'd still have to have contact with Gene it *was*…

She sat up a little straighter in her chair. 'You know I can't refuse. But at the same time I want you to know that I'm only doing this for Philip. If it wasn't for him I *would* refuse. I shouldn't have succumbed to making our association personal.'

Back in bed, when Rose had asserted that she would hold him to his promise to give her anything she wanted, Gene had had a painful moment of disquiet when it had come to him that she might be just like all the other women he'd had liaisons with and see him only as some kind of 'meal ticket' to fame and fortune. But her words and the inflection in her tone now suggested that she felt nothing but regret in meeting him and it cut him to the quick.

It was another first for him. He had never known a woman *willingly* part company with him. Usually the only sensation he experienced when a liaison ended was relief. But with her beguiling violet eyes, and the rare softness that he'd never encountered before, plus the fact that she could turn his blood to molten fire with her presence alone, Rose somehow had him spellbound. So he wouldn't make it at all easy for her to walk away from him—at least not until he'd had his fill of her...

'Good. Then I'd better sign, hadn't I? And I'll need you to witness my signature with your own.'

After the documents had been dealt with, Gene stowed them away in a drawer.

'I'll make sure the money is in your boss's account as soon as you leave,' he affirmed.

'Does that mean I can check the account when I get back to London?' Rose asked warily.

Gene expelled a sigh. 'I may be a lot of things that you don't like, but I never lie about money, Rose. I've got the property that I wanted and I'm not going to delay paying what I owe. An agreement is an agreement.'

They both got to their feet.

'It's nearly time for you to meet the boat. Why don't you go and get your bag and I'll walk you down to the quay?' he suggested.

His companion's soft satin cheeks inexplicably

turned pink. Was she perhaps not as set on leaving as she had indicated? he wondered?

'That won't be necessary,' she answered stiffly, immediately pouring ice water on the thought. 'I'm quite capable of getting there by myself.'

'Damn it, woman. I'm doing it for my own satisfaction. I just want to make sure you get off the island safely. There'll be a car waiting for you on the other side, like I promised. My driver will take you to the airport, and there'll be another driver waiting for you when you land, to take you back home.'

'I'm going to go to the hospital first—to see Philip.'

'Of course you are.' A flash of what felt suspiciously like jealousy at her unerring regard for the other man ricocheted though Gene's insides. 'I'll meet you out at the front. Go and get your bag.'

A mournful wind was howling as they started to walk down the hillside and, glancing at the ocean, he saw that the surging waves had a chilling bluish tint and were far from calm. The scent of last night's storm still clung to the icy air and he shivered.

Unable to help himself, he hoped that the conditions were too rough this morning for Rory to make the crossing. But then he quickly realised that even if the boatman was able to make the journey to the island there was no guarantee that the return journey would be any smoother.

Suddenly Gene didn't want to let Rose go. If anything happened to her when he could have taken steps to prevent it he'd never forgive himself.

'It looks rougher than usual out there today,' he remarked, coming to a sudden standstill on the uneven stone path to survey his windblown companion.

Her expression impatient, Rose tried in vain to push her fringe out of her eyes. 'It must be because of the storm. I'm sure it will be all right. Rory strikes me as a highly competent boatman.'

'Even the most competent sailors still have to contend with the unpredictable nature of the ocean,' he said dryly. 'Why don't we go back? I'll see if I can contact him and tell him that you'll wait until

tomorrow, when the weather will hopefully be a bit calmer.'

'*No.*'

Agitated and furious, Rose turned away and started to make her way down the hillside. Her leather tote bumped awkwardly against her side as she gamely negotiated the uneven rocky surface. She'd adamantly refused to let Gene carry it for her.

'The sooner I get off this island the better!' she shouted back over her shoulder.

Too concerned for her safety to let her head off without him, in just a few long-legged strides he had joined her. 'I hadn't realised how stubborn you are, but I'm quickly learning,' he murmured.

'If you mean that I know my own mind, and won't let anyone dictate what I should or shouldn't do, then, yes—I *am* stubborn.' With a flash of sublime violet and a bewitching satisfied smile, Rose forged ahead to the carved-out landing stage in the bay where the boat would dock.

She got there before him, her back straight in her

weatherproof jacket and hanging on to her tote for dear life in the unforgiving gusting wind. She stared defiantly out to sea, as if fully expecting Rory's boat to appear on the horizon any moment now just because she *willed* it…

CHAPTER SEVEN

THE MEMORY OF Gene calling out, 'I'll be in touch soon!' as Rory steered the boat back out of the bay haunted Rose for several nights after she'd returned to London. The exclamation could so easily have sounded like a threat—but it *hadn't*. Instead she'd sensed regret in his tone, as if he genuinely hadn't wanted her to leave.

She'd watched the disturbingly lonely figure he'd made on the shoreline until he had become a mere speck in the distance that had quickly disappeared. It had left a hollow feeling inside her that was hard to explain.

But her spirits had lifted when she'd discovered that Philip had made some definite improvement while she'd been away. And when she'd given him the news that Gene had officially bought the building and the antiques, and that the money was now safely in his bank account, the worried expression Rose had become used to seeing on a daily basis had started to fade. He'd even seemed to breathe a little more easily.

Having returned to work, her aim was to finish meticulously cataloguing the antiques and then to make contact with the dealers and auctioneers she knew who would be interested and hopefully make some sales. There was still the odd 'walk in' buyer that came into the store, and she didn't mind—she'd always loved conversing with customers. But the fact was that her job was swiftly coming to an end and she was now in effect working for Gene instead of Philip.

It was a twist of fate that she couldn't have predicted...not even in her wildest dreams.

She had just got off the phone one afternoon when the bell above the door jangled to announce a visitor. Glad of the distraction, Rose left the office to see who it was. It had been an agonisingly slow day, and she had spent most of her time trying to persuade a wealthy dealer in Paris to visit the shop and view a valuable chiffonier that she knew was right up his street. Sometimes it wasn't enough simply to view an item online. A true connoisseur had to physically see and touch the artefact.

The Parisian dealer was known for his exquisite good taste, and the fact that this piece had originated in the French capital was all to the good. Its provenance was impeccable. Rose had assured him that she would foot the bill for the trip—at the back of her mind she'd told herself that Gene couldn't possibly mind as long as she secured the deal and the chiffonier was sold. After all, wasn't making a profit his main concern?

The moment she walked out onto the shop floor and saw it was Gene himself standing there, his arms ominously folded across his broad chest, devastatingly suited in flawless tailoring as if he was going on to some important business function, her heart clamoured wildly and suddenly her ability to know what to say utterly deserted her.

Clearly not sharing her dilemma, he said smoothly, 'I thought I'd drop by and see how things were going.'

He was acting as if this was the usual way he did business—simply dropping by unannounced. Didn't he have a secretary or some smartly dressed snooty PA to do his bidding? Of course he did. Hadn't Rose spoken to the woman herself when she'd requested a meeting with him? And, yes, the woman *had* sounded snooty...

Clearing her throat, she shakily combed her fingers through her hair. Not since early this morning had she even glanced in a mirror to see how she looked. She couldn't even remember applying any make-up. Telling herself that she shouldn't care how she appeared to Gene, she knew the truth was that she cared more than was probably wise...

'By that I assume you want to know how the sales are getting on? I'm sure you're anxious to have the building emptied and renovated as soon as possible.'

A maddeningly inexplicable smile played round his lips. 'Of course I'm interested to hear how many antiques you've sold on my behalf—but that's not the sole reason for my visit, Rose. I came to see how you were.'

'No doubt you were wondering if I've recovered from my ordeal on the island. It's certainly an experience I'll never forget. That was some lightning storm, wasn't it? Well, I'm still alive and kicking—as you can see.'

'That's not what I meant. We didn't exactly part on the best of terms, did we? I'd hate to think you were still angry with me.'

'I'm not. Tensions were high because of what we'd both been through…that's all.'

'Well, I missed you after you'd left. I came back the next day because the place was too empty without you.'

Rose's heart skipped a beat. *What was he playing at, making such a provocative statement?*

'Isn't that the purpose of having a sanctuary? So that you can be alone and hopefully enjoy some peace?'

Gene grimaced, and it wasn't the reaction she'd expected. It took her aback to see the pain that had momentarily flared in his dazzling blue eyes.

'There's never any peace when you're alone with your thoughts…at least that's been my experience.'

Such a frank and very *human* confession took Rose aback once more. The world seemed to be of the opinion that a man like Gene who had everything—could have anything he wanted at the drop of a hat—was devoid of any human feelings at all. His desire for more went beyond reason, it seemed. Wasn't that how *she* had viewed him? But it had slowly crept up on her that there was far more to him than that. And, in spite of her fears about being used by him, she realised she wanted to know *more* about him…not *less*.

'I know what you mean. Thoughts can drive us crazy sometimes, can't they? Look, I was just about to make a cup of tea before you appeared. Would you like one?'

The frown that creased his indomitable brow immediately relaxed and the smile he gave her seemed perfectly genuine. 'If you could make that coffee and not tea…that would be great.'

'Coffee it is, then. We'll take it into the office.'

Gene couldn't help recalling the last time he'd been in Philip Houghton's office. He winced when he remembered how his meeting with Rose had ended. Had he intuited even at that early stage of their acquaintance that she was going to shake up his world as it had never been shaken before? With her bewitching violet eyes, and the stubborn way she had of refusing to give in to his wants and needs, she was unlike any other woman he'd known before.

The fact that she seemed far from impressed by his wealth and status, and wasn't readily going to succumb to his charms, made her even more desirable. How would she react if he confessed that he hadn't been able to stop thinking about their impassioned lovemaking on the island? That since he'd tasted her soft cherry lips and intimately known her body she'd infiltrated his blood like a contagious fever that bordered on dangerous…at least to his state of mind?

He had even been finding it hard to concentrate on work—and that was unheard of.

Now, as she sat opposite him on the other side of the desk, Gene thought she looked a little flushed. Her short dark hair was mussed, as if she'd been frequently running her fingers through it because she was stressed… or worried… He didn't particularly want to discuss her boss, but he would have to if he wanted to learn what was troubling her.

'How is Mr Houghton?' he enquired, endeavouring to keep his tone as amiable as possible.

'Better than I hoped.'

'You mean he's rallying?'

'Yes. He's by no means recovered, but the doctors tell me he's definitely made some improvement. Knowing that he's sold the antiques store and no longer has the worry of paying for his aftercare when he comes out of hospital has definitely helped.'

'That's good. But what about *you*, Rose?'

'What do you mean?'

'I mean you look like something's bothering you. What are you worrying about if it's not your boss's state of health?'

Breathing out a sigh, she sat a little further back in her seat. 'I'm not *worried*. I'm…concerned. Concerned that it's going to take me quite some time to sell all these antiques and that in the meantime I need to find a new job.'

The opportunity that Gene had hoped would come his way had just landed straight in his lap… Pausing to reflect on his good fortune, he smiled and took a leisurely sip of his coffee.

'You don't need to look for a new job. You're working for *me* now—remember?' he reminded her.

The compellingly beautiful violet eyes widened. 'I know you're paying me to source buyers for the antiques on your behalf, but it's hardly a full-time position, is it?'

'No, it's not. That being the case, I'm sure I can find you something suitable in one of my companies.'

Rose looked at him aghast. 'Like *what*, for instance?'

'Something in the administration area, perhaps… I'm assuming your organisational skills are good?'

'But I'm not an administrator, am I? I'm an antiques dealer.'

Crossly she folded her arms over her very neat crimson sweater. The fitted cashmere garment couldn't fail to highlight her beautifully shaped breasts and tiny waist, and Gene hotly sensed his hunger to make love to her again becoming an undeniable craving he couldn't resist for very much longer...

She lifted her chin. 'In any case, I don't want you to find me a job. I'm quite capable of doing that for myself.'

His thoughts were racing, and he couldn't prevent his growing frustration from spilling over into his tone. 'Do you know how many résumés my offices receive every day? On average about a hundred. Most people would give their eye teeth for the opportunity to work for me!'

'Well, good luck to them—but I'm not one of those.' Lifting her cup to her lips, she took a brief sip of her tea and clattered the vessel against the matching porcelain saucer when she set it down again.

He didn't miss the fact that her hand was shaking. *God, the woman was stubborn!* He longed for her to relent a little. He found himself momentarily lost in the memory of touching her breasts, and of the way her tender nipples had instantly hardened and contracted against his hand...

He stood up, because he suddenly couldn't stay still, and walked round the desk to study her more closely.

'I'd like to let you go so that you can look for a job you really want, but I'm afraid I can't. What I *can* do, however, is double the fee I'm paying you so that you won't have any worries about money until you find a new position. Does that make things easier for you?'

'It's not just about the money…'

'You don't *want* to stay and sell the antiques for me? Is that what you're saying?'

'It's just too awkward…'

'Why?'

'Because I've worked all these years for *Philip*—and you're not him!'

Her upsurge of emotion took them both by surprise. Rose was breathing hard and chewing anxiously down on her fulsome lower lip and Gene's heart was thudding fit to burst. Her meaning was clear. The thought that she regarded the aging antiques dealer over him made his blood boil. He knew he had no reason to be jealous, because she'd made it clear to him that her devotion to the man was purely out of respect and kindness, but he couldn't help feeling the way he did.

Reaching down, he furiously pulled her to her feet. 'You're sorry that I'm not some elderly English gentleman who couldn't give you even *one* night of pleasure if he tried?'

He brought his face down to hers and felt her slender frame tremble.

'That's the most ridiculous notion I've ever heard. If you met him you'd know why. He's the sweetest, kindest man I've ever met and I've already told you I'm not remotely attracted to him.'

Gene heard the heartfelt words but was too far gone to be remotely gracious. He was lost in an incandescent violet sea and in a sweet perfume so seductive that he was helpless to resist the erotic delights it promised. He crushed Rose's luscious cherry lips beneath his without an ounce of remorse and devoured them.

At some point during his greedy exploration he tasted blood on his lips and didn't know whether it was his or hers. But then, incredibly, he realised that she was kissing him back—that she'd freed her hands and was hungrily urging him closer. At the same time she was making breathless little sounds that told him she wanted and needed him as much as he did her...

His blood pounding hotly in his veins, Gene acknowledged that the sparks they'd helplessly ignited together had suddenly caught fire. And there was only one solution to dousing the flames—and that was to unrestrainedly let them *burn*...

With a heated groan he swept aside all the paraphernalia on the desk and papers and items of stationery fell haphazardly onto the floor. His gaze briefly colliding with Rose's, he gripped her arms and, as gently as he was able, helped her to lie back on the mahogany surface.

She was already pushing his suit jacket aside and urgently opening his shirt buttons so that she could touch him. When she ran her hands over his chest and round his ribcage it was an irresistible combination of heaven and hell for Gene. Heaven because being close to her in this way was beyond his wildest dreams as far as pleasure was concerned, and hell because he was so turned on it was painful...

Capturing her mouth in a hard, hot kiss, he dragged up the hem of her skirt to find her panties. When his hands fastened round the skimpy white silk that adorned her svelte hips he eagerly pulled down the garment to mid-thigh and urgently undid his zip. He was almost beyond aching to be inside her.

When Rose clasped her velvet thighs around him he needed no further invitation. He plunged his inflamed sex deep inside her moist satin centre. They both stilled for a moment—not in shock or surprise, but in wonder at the unbelievable ecstasy of their union. Then Gene's ability to think even close to straight disappeared as he was driven to thrust even deeper, at the same time pushing aside her sweater and bra to fasten his mouth on a sweetly distended nipple, nibbling at it with the edges of his teeth.

The taste of her was like the sweetest nectar imaginable and he was already addicted to it. Since their very first combustible encounter Gene had known he wouldn't easily be able to relinquish sampling it again and again…

Releasing a sensuous moan, Rose suddenly stilled beneath him.

Raising his head to glance down at her, he saw that her beautiful eyes looked startled. He saw too that the incandescent violet orbs were glazed with moisture and that it had darkened the fringe of ebony lashes that surrounded them. He didn't pause to wonder why she should shed a tear at such a pleasurable moment because he was already a mere breath away from the climactic fulfilment of his own sensual journey.

In the next instant his desire reached its zenith and his entire body vibrated with the power of it. Releasing a guttural groan that might have emanated from the undiscovered corners of his very soul, Gene lowered his head to rest it against Rose's chest. If they had been in bed together he would have gathered her into his arms and held her for the longest time. Yet again a strong wave of protectiveness had swept over him, and he couldn't help but want to express it.

He was just about to enquire if she was all right, and tell her how beautiful she was, when the lyrical sound of the shop's doorbell made them both stiffen in alarm.

'It must be a customer...' Rose said huskily, her hands already pushing him away.

Even as she spoke Gene cursed beneath his breath, hurriedly got to his feet and tidied his disarrayed clothing.

Red-faced, Rose gave him a nervous glance as she straightened her skirt and tucked in her sweater. Then she dragged her fingers through her mussed hair and went to the door.

Turning, she said, 'If you go through that door you'll find a cloakroom where you can freshen up. I'll tell whoever it is that I'm closing early today.'

'Good idea,' he muttered.

When she'd closed the door behind her he cursed again—not because they'd been interrupted, but because in the throes of a passion that had been as fierce and elemental as the lightning storm they'd witnessed on the island he'd stupidly omitted to use protection...

The unexpected caller turned out to be the persistently cheerful postman, who had once told Rose that his name was Bill. He was making a late delivery, he explained, due to the 'horrendous traffic'.

Rose didn't usually mind a bit of a chat with him, but not today...

Not when she'd left Gene in the office, waiting for her.

The explosion of passion that had erupted between them had made her head spin. There wasn't an inch of flesh on her body that didn't throb and ache, and she was pretty sure she'd inadvertently acquired a couple of bruises. *They'd made love on the office desk, for goodness' sake!* Had she completely taken leave of her senses?

It stunned her that she'd been so reckless. But at the same time, strangely, she felt no regret. In fact she didn't feel like the woman she'd always known herself to be at all...that was someone who always strove to do what was right and act accordingly. She felt like a woman who had somehow liberated herself from the yoke of conformity that had more or less dominated her whole life because of the way she'd been raised—and the feeling was *beyond* exhilarating...

And, although she still found it hard to trust, Gene was the one responsible for her liberation. In his arms she could believe that *anything* was possible.

Bill handed over the pile of letters he'd brought and commented, 'By the way, have you seen that top-of-the-range black Mercedes in the car park? Presumably it belongs to one of your rich customers? It's got a personal number plate...reads EB1. Got any idea who that might be?'

Excruciatingly, Rose felt herself redden. She endeavoured to make her answer sound as uninterested as possible. 'No, I don't. It probably belongs to someone who's popped into the bank. Anyway, thanks for the post. I've got to get on now. I'm shutting up shop early today.'

'Got a hot date, have you?' Bill gave her a playful wink.

Wincing, Rose went behind him to the door and pointedly held it open.

'All right, love, I can take a hint!' He smiled. 'See you next time!'

Breathing a sigh of relief when he was gone, she locked the door and turned the sign that hung there round to read 'Closed'. Then she smoothed down her newly wrinkled smart black skirt and prepared herself to return to the office and face the man who had had no compunction in making her his lover yet again...

CHAPTER EIGHT

WHEN SHE RETURNED to the office it was to find Eugene disappearing through the back door to locate the cloakroom. The papers and stationery he'd swept onto the floor had been returned to the desk and arranged tidily. Anyone stepping into the room would not notice anything remotely amiss. They certainly wouldn't guess that Rose and a well-known billionaire had been making out on the desk!

Walking across the room to her chair, she feverishly reflected on what had happened. She couldn't still her trembling as she sat down. Anguished, she murmured aloud, 'What have I done?'

In the aftermath of the event, shock had set in. Not just shock, but guilt and a generous portion of shame too. *What would Philip think if he knew? What would her father have said if he'd been alive?* Rose felt as if she'd let them both down. But, more importantly, she'd also let *herself* down. There was a good reason why she'd always sought to behave well. When her parents had split her father's friends had intimated that her mother, Ruth, had had a 'wild streak' that her father had never really come to terms with.

Philip had once shared with Rose that her father had told him, 'Living with that woman was like building a house on top of a repository for dynamite. Not a day went by when I didn't anticipate it might blow up in my face.'

Ruth Heathcote had caused utter devastation when she'd deserted him for the wealthy and flamboyant David Carlisle. He'd been absolutely crushed by her leaving and had gone to court to make sure that Rose was raised by him and not her... Suffering the fall-out of those painful events had made Rose determined never to behave as recklessly.

But she was well aware that when nature held sway humans were more often than not powerless to resist. That was why she'd ended up in bed with Gene at the sanctuary. Yet her self-respect was paramount, and she wouldn't jeopardise that if she could help it... *Or so she'd believed.* What she hadn't been prepared for was a man like Gene Bonnaire sweeping into her life and leaving her feeling as though she'd just survived a tornado by the skin of her teeth.

And now there was something else she'd better keep in mind. They had been intimate without even giving a thought to using protection. They'd been so mesmerised by their urgent feelings that it hadn't even crossed their minds. At least Rose knew that Gene hadn't *planned* the passionate seduction. If he had, he would most definitely have brought protection. He might flirt with danger in his business life, but she was certain a man like him wouldn't take unnecessary risks in his personal one...

Although it would be easy to give way to panic, she absolutely refused to. Thankfully, she knew all about the morning-after pill, and before she went home she would go straight to a pharmacy. An unplanned pregnancy was something that definitely *wasn't* in her plans for the future...

Gene returned. The expression on his handsome face was a little shame-faced. To counteract it, a tentative smile lifted a corner of his sculpted lips and Rose's senses were immediately assailed by the seductive scent of him. In her chair, she couldn't help but clench her thighs together. Her heart raced when she thought how desperately they had made love. In his arms she had learned what it meant to be ecstatic, freed of restriction. It had felt like *flying*...

'Who was your visitor? A potential customer?' he enquired.

As he asked the question he was walking slowly towards her, and she had ample time to admire his hard, honed physique in the impeccable bespoke suit. If Gene didn't flirt with danger in *his* personal life, then Rose knew that was *exactly* what she'd be doing in hers if she didn't tell him that turning their association into a sexual one had been a bad mistake. As much as the thought grieved her, the two hot little encounters they'd enjoyed wouldn't be happening again.

'It was the postman making a late delivery,' she told him.

'His timing could have been better.'

Rose flushed. 'He said that the traffic was bad. That's why he got held up.'

'Never mind about that... I'm more interested in what *we're* doing. I want you to come back with me to my apartment tonight. This time I want to make sure I have you all to myself. I don't want to risk our time together being interrupted again.'

He was drawing her to her feet as he spoke and his arms were wound firmly round her waist.

Finding herself once again mesmerised by his cobalt blue eyes and fit body, so soon after the intimacy they'd shared, Rose sensed her determination to hold him at bay and deny him any further intimate contact teeter precariously.

'That might be what *you* want, Gene, but it's not what *I* want.'

'I don't believe you.'

He had the temerity to look amused, and she couldn't help but take umbrage. Flattening her hands against his shirtfront, she pushed him away...or at least she *tried* to push him away.

He wasn't having any of it and held her fast.

'Look, I might have agreed to *temporarily* do a job for you,' she reminded him, 'but that doesn't mean I've agreed to be at your beck and call day and night.'

'Did I say that's what I wanted?' He sighed, and his warm breath fanned her face. 'Neither would I want to be at *your* beck and call day and night, Rose. But if we need to spend some time together that's a different proposition entirely...wouldn't you say?'

Noting that he had said *need* instead of *want* sent a

traitorous warm glow pulsing through Rose. The declaration didn't make it sound as if he intended to use her and then cast her aside so he could go on to the next available woman he took a fancy to.

And yet the memory of her ex Joe's behaviour reminded her that she shouldn't give her trust so easily —she couldn't afford to be lulled into a false sense of security by the dangerous hope that Gene genuinely wanted to have a relationship with her. Didn't his much-documented brief liaisons with various models and actresses prove that he wasn't a man who believed in long-term relationships?

'I just don't think it's a good idea for us to spend any more time together…at least not in *that* way. From now on our relationship should be a purely professional one. I'll do what you're paying me to do as regards selling the antiques, but there'll be no need for us to associate outside of work.'

'I disagree.'

'I thought you might—but that's only because you want your own way. My mind is made up, Gene.'

'And what if you find out you're pregnant?'

He came back at her like a whip and his gaze was suddenly ominously cold. Rose shivered, but he still didn't release her.

'You don't have to worry about that.'

'You mean you're on the pill?'

'No. But there's a morning-after pill I can get from the pharmacy that inhibits ovulation. I'm going to get it on the way home.'

'So I don't have any say in the matter at all?'

'I thought you'd be pleased that there's something we can do. I'm sure you don't want to be tied to me because of a child we created in a totally crazy moment of unforeseen passion.'

For a perturbing few moments Gene didn't know what to say. Everything in him felt as though it had been shaken up and displaced—and, worse than that, he sensed it wasn't likely that the various parts would be returned to their original positions any time soon…

Then he remembered what had instigated their 'crazy moment of unforeseen passion'. He'd told Rose that she was working for *him* now, and she hadn't seemed at all happy. She had finished by exclaiming 'But you're not him!' as if she mourned the fact that he wasn't her boss, Philip Houghton.

His arms locked even tighter round her impossibly small waist. An undeniable sense of ownership and possession seized him. 'Are you intent on taking this morning-after pill because you don't trust me? Do you think I wouldn't take responsibility?'

Rose sighed. 'I haven't thought about anything much beyond protecting myself. We're not in a serious relationship and I'm equally responsible for what just happened. I'm just being sensible.'

'Why? Has something like this happened to you before? You indicated once that you'd been hurt by someone.'

'I was. But he didn't make me pregnant and abandon me, if that's what you were thinking. In a way what he did was worse than that. He fooled around behind my back and then lied about it as if it was nothing.'

Even though she'd endeavoured to make her tone sound matter-of-fact, Gene still heard the pain in her voice. He felt as though he'd been punched. The thought of a man regularly cheating on Rose and then lying to her instigated that primitive impulse in him to protect and defend her honour.

'I'm sorry you had to go through that,' he said, low-voiced, 'but that's not the way *I* behave. You're well rid of the jerk. Getting back to the present situation, I know you're being practical in thinking about a morning-after pill, but what about our feelings? Don't *they* come into the equation at all?'

Gene's heart was galloping as he heard himself asking the one question he'd never asked a woman before. But since meeting Rose he was being more and more drawn to acknowledge an area of his life that he'd long ago become adept at turning away from... *his emotions.*

The matchless violet gaze in front of him reflected her alarm. 'Are you seriously telling me that you have some kind of—of *feeling* about the possibility of me having a baby?'

'I'm not completely heartless. There are some things in life that cause a person to stop and think. A possible pregnancy is one of them.'

'But I've already told you—it's not just your responsibility.'

'I hear you. But I also want you to hear *me*, Rose. I don't know how or why, but we seem to have developed some kind of connection—a connection that's a little deeper than run of the mill. It's not something I want to ignore, and neither do I want to just put it down to experience.'

'I hardly know what to say…'

'In that case there's absolutely no reason why we can't make our relationship more personal, is there?'

'Didn't we just make it about as personal as it can be?'

Rose's comment was clearly meant to be ironic. Unfortunately Gene saw no reason for humour—ironic or otherwise…

He unceremoniously released her. Scraping his fingers through his perfectly groomed hair, he was intensely frustrated that she didn't seem to want to take their relationship more seriously. Even though they'd been intimate, it was easy to sense that she was already putting up walls between them… *He wished he could knock every one of them down.*

Having never experienced a woman spurning him before, he barely knew what to do. Already he felt bereft because she wasn't in his arms… He could flex his masculinity and *insist* she came home with him, but this was the twenty-first century and Rose was an independent woman. He sensed she wouldn't take at all well to his throwing his weight around. In fact, such an action would probably drive her away completely. He would have to mull over another strategy.

Meeting her gaze, he said, 'If you won't come back to my apartment then why don't you let me drive you home?'

'There's no need. I can get the bus—like I usually do.'

'You don't drive?'

'No…I don't.'

In that volatile moment he couldn't contain his temper that things weren't going his way, and he snapped, 'Then go and get yourself ready and I'll meet you out front in my car. Our first destination will be the pharmacy…'

Rose was exiting the pharmacy and heading towards the luxurious Mercedes that waited for her outside when a man with a camera rushed towards her. Pointing it at her, he was taking continuous snaps even as he moved.

'Are you Eugene Bonnaire's new girlfriend? What's your name, love? You might as well tell me. I saw his car. What other reason would he have for parking it there?'

Even as she reeled with shock she saw Gene hurriedly open the door next to the driver's seat. Rose registered the furious muscle that flexed in his hard-chiselled jaw.

He yelled, 'Get in the car quickly and don't tell that idiot anything!'

Rose moved almost without thinking. She all but threw herself into the luxuriously upholstered passenger seat and Gene started the engine as she was still closing the door. The precision-engineered car moved smoothly away from the kerb.

'That's exactly what I *don't* need,' he murmured.

Placing her bag down by her feet, she glanced up. 'I wouldn't have said anything, you know. I certainly wouldn't have given him my name. Does that kind of thing happen very often?'

'A little too often for my liking… I never thought I'd miss my anonymity, but it's funny how things change.'

Genuinely surprised that he should share such a personal reflection, Rose relaxed a little. Perhaps Gene didn't seek the limelight as much as the press made out that he did? Could that be the reason he'd looked so unhappy in that photo she'd seen of him at the awards ceremony? The idea of having your every move stalked and being photographed by paparazzi must be a living nightmare. There was nothing about his life that she remotely envied. In fact she suddenly found herself feeling genuinely sad for his lack of privacy...

'I never thought I'd say this, but I feel for you, Gene...I really do. I'm glad I said we should keep our relationship on a professional footing rather than a personal one. In light of events like *that* happening, it's probably best if you stay away. We can communicate by phone.'

Turning his head towards her, he scowled. 'I won't be dictated to by anybody—least of all the media.' He returned his furious gaze to the road. 'Just give me your address and I'll take you home.'

When they pulled up outside the neat semi-detached house in the pleasant cul-de-sac where Rose lived, Gene switched off the engine and turned to gaze out of the window at the building. Rose saw him glance at the newly mown lawn and the tidy window boxes that were full of colourful perennials. It was late autumn, and she loved the fact that they were still in bloom. But he was probably thinking how ordinary the place was, she reflected.

'Have you always lived here?' he asked.

Even as she nodded, she hated the feeling that he

might be judging her in some way because of where she lived.

'It's the house I grew up in with my parents. When my father died he left it to me.'

'Not your mother?'

She shook her head. 'No. They weren't together any more.'

'You mean they were divorced?'

Expelling a jaundiced sigh, Rose replied, 'Yes. She ran off with a rich unscrupulous businessman who promised her a better life.' She couldn't hide the bitterness in her tone and sensed her cheeks flush red.

Gene's brow puckered interestedly. 'And *did* he…? Give her a better life, I mean?'

'Depends what you mean by "better". As far as I know she's happy. They live in a swanky place in Paris and she doesn't want for anything. Apparently she's got the kind of life she always dreamt of…the kind of life that my father could never have afforded to give her. But she broke his heart when she left him and he never really recovered.'

'I'm sorry to hear that. But her desertion must have been tough on you too?'

Rose felt the backs of her eyes sting. 'It was for a while. But then I got over it. I had to deal with what was in front of me. In any case, who needs a mother who'd rather have the material things in life over the people that really love her?'

She thought she saw Gene wince.

'What did he do for a living? I mean your father?' he asked.

'He was an accountant…a very good one, as a matter of fact.' She was quite aware that she sounded defensive. 'But he was never as ambitious as my mother wanted him to be. Instead of seeing what a loyal and devoted husband and father he was, she saw the fact that he put spending time with his family before rising in his career as a weakness.'

'You said that your mother and her husband live in Paris? Can you tell me where?'

Again Rose sensed her face heat. She didn't doubt that Gene would know the place. She hadn't forgotten that he was French. 'It's a suburb called Neuilly-sur-Seine.'

'If they can afford to live there he *must* be rich. It's got some of the most prime real estate in the city.'

She shrugged and unbuckled her seatbelt. 'I wouldn't know. Nor do I care.'

Before she could turn and open the car door she heard the soft snick of Gene's seatbelt being freed. Leaning towards her, he captured her hand and held it fast.

'Before you go I think we need to have a serious talk, don't you?'

Like a moth drawn to a flame, she fell headlong into the dangerous fire of his glittering blue gaze and sensed herself sizzle. At the same time the sensual musky scent of him made her insides melt. Shockingly, all she could think about was the silkily hard, hot sensation of him inside her… It stunned Rose just how much she ached to experience his intimate possession again.

She bit down hard on the lower lip that was already contused from his passionate kisses. 'What kind of a talk? If it's about the sale of the antiques I told you I'd stay in touch.'

Even to her own ears her voice sounded distinctly shaky.

'You know damn well it's not about the antiques. We need to talk about what just happened between us at the shop.'

Rose forced herself to stay strong, not to let him suspect how deeply his passionate attentions had affected her. 'We had sex on my boss's desk…that's what happened. I told you I was going to take the morning-after pill to make sure I don't get pregnant, so you don't have to worry. What else do we need to talk about?'

'I don't believe for one second that's *all* you think we did, Rose.'

Suddenly Gene was lifting her hand towards his lips with strangely purposeful intent…

'We made *fire* back there—that's what we did…a fire that burned us both right down to our core. And if you deny it I won't hesitate to call you a liar.'

Even as he made the assertion he was inserting her slender forefinger into the silkily hot cavern of his mouth and sucking it…

She gasped. 'What are you…? What are you doing?' She snatched her hand away even as she wished that she was brave enough to keep it there.

His lips formed a lazily knowing smile. 'I was reacquainting myself with your taste, Rose. It seems that I can't get enough of it.'

'Well, you're going to have to learn to do without it— because I can't and won't continue with this stupidity!'

The feeling that she was about to burst into tears was overwhelming. Because she didn't want to make an even bigger fool of herself than she'd done already, she snatched up her bag and opened the door.

As she stepped out onto the pavement Gene's inscrutable handsome features gave not the slightest clue as to his feelings, but he remarked, 'You might call it stupidity for us to spend more time together, Rose, but I don't happen to share that view. Whatever the outcome of this situation, I personally have no regrets. Be assured that I'll be in touch.'

Rose didn't reply. Instead she slammed the car door shut and headed straight for the house. Even as she heard him pull away, and as the tears she'd tried so hard to hold back started to stream down her face, she made sure not to turn and follow his progress…

CHAPTER NINE

GENE HADN'T BEEN lying when he'd commented to Rose that he couldn't get enough of her taste. It wasn't just her taste he was addicted to either. He couldn't get enough of *her*…especially since that wild episode in Philip's office. His blood rushed and his heart pumped harder every time he thought about it.

The realisation that she was becoming more important to him than he'd ever envisaged threatened everything. Dear God, the woman had him in such a tailspin he'd barely even given the ownership of the antiques shop building a thought. How could that be? he wondered. Wasn't possession of the listed building supposed to be the icing on the cake, crowning yet another successful year of his restaurant chain as well as the other numerous lucrative investments he'd made?

It didn't feel like that. It made him realise there was a big difference between *being* successful and *feeling* successful—and right then he didn't feel successful at all. He felt strangely empty…as though everything he'd set such store by in his life had suddenly become meaningless.

Rose's story about her mother's desertion of her for an 'unscrupulous rich businessman' had definitely hit a nerve. It was evident that she despised her stepfather. Without a doubt Gene could probably find at least a dozen parallels with himself and the man, and it was quite possible he even *knew* him. The business community *he* was a member of only welcomed the 'elite of the elite' into their ranks…the wealthiest and most powerful of men and women…and Rose's stepfather might even be one of Gene's competitors.

Yet it wasn't that that perturbed him. It was the knowledge that he'd behaved exactly like her mother when he'd turned his back on his loved ones, believing that the simple life his parents enjoyed wasn't enough. He'd become greedy and ambitious, and hearing Rose's story had made him aware of some of the more negative consequences his desires had wrought.

He'd purchased a beautiful Georgian house for his parents a few years ago and had sensed their deep unease at accepting it.

His father had told him, 'It's a wonderful gift, son, but in truth your mother and me would rather know that you're happy and content, and have your company from time to time, than have you buy us a house. We're quite happy with our simple little terrace. All our memories are here…it's where we raised you and your sister.'

Gene had felt crass and insensitive. He'd never even considered what *they* wanted. Yet it hurt him deeply that they'd never understood how much losing his beloved sister, Francesca, had affected *him*. Knowing that life was so precarious and ephemeral had really shaken him. And the need to protect his remaining family at all costs had driven him to become more and more successful in the world. Yet he had never been able to share his feelings with them about it.

After the disappointing reception of his well-meant gift of the house he had retreated to lick his wounds and had distanced himself from them even more. Gene had numbed his discomfort and pain by acquiring even more restaurants and playing the stock market. He had been employing the only way he knew how to protect himself from further hurt.

He had been as devastated as his parents when illness had so cruelly taken Francesca from them. From time to time her beautiful face would come into his mind, and it was like a knife in his heart that he would never see her grow into a woman, would never see her fall in love, maybe marry and have children of her own...

They'd all been like ghosts after she went...alive, but not really living. And now Gene feared he'd lost his parents' respect and regard. They might tell him that they loved him, but too often when he visited he saw pain and disappointment in their eyes because of the path he'd taken. They had no idea what drove him to pursue success and money so relentlessly and probably never would. They no doubt believed it made him happy. How could they know what a high price he paid for being so driven?

Every night when he went home from his day's work—to his apartment in London or either of the desirable residences he owned in New York and Paris when he was there—more often than not he went home alone. Eugene didn't have relationships. He had joyless liaisons that were usually conducted in some luxurious hotel that was utterly devoid of anything remotely homely or comforting. It made him secretly despise the women he entertained, because they were more interested in his money than in expressing even a passing interest in the real man behind the wealthy and polished veneer...

He might have been kidding himself that that was okay, but deep down he knew it was a *lie*. Seeing Rose's house today, in an ordinary suburban cul-de-sac, with its well-tended window boxes and tidily perfect lawn, he had been almost *envious* that she clearly didn't feel the need for something grander. The mere concept of being satisfied with your lot in life was a million miles away from the world Gene inhabited. And, although he couldn't envisage himself in a similar situation to hers, it had surprisingly instilled in him a longing for some of the comforts of a real home.

And it wasn't just that that he longed to experience.

There was a deep yearning inside him to be with someone who really cared...someone who didn't just want him for what he could provide materially but who genuinely wanted to get to know him and likewise would let him get to know *her*...

He headed for the kitchen. Whenever he was troubled and—yes—sometimes *sickened* by the relentless desire for more that had set him apart from so much that was true, he returned to the one thing that was guaranteed to give him pleasure...*cooking*. And while he gathered together the pots, pans and ingredients that he needed to make a meal his thoughts inevitably turned to Rose and the meal he'd made for her on the island.

Already it had become one of Gene's favourite memories. But thinking of her was bittersweet, because he'd left her on her own to deal with the possibility that he might have made her pregnant. *It wasn't right.* He hated the idea that she might be feeling scared and upset. Having the presence of mind to think about taking the morning-after pill might denote that she was a practical woman, but he knew she was a sensitive one too.

Frustrated that he couldn't be with her, he reached for his mobile and dialled the number of a trusted business colleague who was the owner of an exclusive jeweller's in Bond Street. After that he contacted an equally prestigious florist. If he couldn't have the pleasure of Rose's company tonight at least he could do something to show her that he cared about the compromising situation he had put her in…

The next morning Rose was roused from a restless night with very little sleep to take unexpected delivery of the most beautiful bouquet of white roses. Even as she carefully transported them into the kitchen to put them into her favourite crystal vase the scent of the flowers filled the air like a soporific hypnotic balm. Had Philip sent them to thank her for dealing with the sale of the antiques store?

With their exotic scent and lush, velvety petals, even in her sleep-deprived state they couldn't help but make Rose think of Cleopatra, Queen of the Nile. The legend went that the queen had regularly bathed in a bath of milk scented with rose petals…

Gently laying the bouquet down on the table, she bent to inhale the scent a little more closely. It was then that she saw the card that accompanied them, and tucked in amongst the flowers she saw a narrow red velvet box. Frowning, she opened the card and studied the inscription. With her pulse racing she read it.

To the Hidden Diamond I never expected to find.
Gene x.

Gene had sent her the flowers? To receive such a message from him was so unexpected, so exhilarating, that Rose felt quite intoxicated by it.

Pulling out a chair from the table, she sank down into it because her legs suddenly felt as though they might not support her. Her mind was racing as she strove to find an explanation of what he might mean. Then she reached into the bouquet of buttery roses for the glamorous presentation box. She opened it.

Lying on a bed of sumptuous cream silk was the most dazzling diamond bracelet Rose had ever seen. Set in white gold, the square-cut gems were flawlessly pristine and glinted up at her like brilliant sunlight radiated through a prism. What had Gene meant by sending her such an amazing and valuable gift?

Lifting the bracelet out of the box, she tried it on. It was blissfully cool against her skin and yet her whole body felt drenched with heat, just thinking about the man who'd sent it. But it was the words he'd written on the card that had taken her aback the most. *The Hidden Diamond...* Was Gene saying that *Rose* was the hidden diamond he'd never expected to find? Was the sentiment a heartfelt one or was he merely flattering her?

She suddenly felt like crying, because more than anything she wanted to believe that Gene meant every word...

The telephone rang. Rose rushed to answer it in case it might be the hospital. As far as Philip's health was concerned he was by no means out of the woods yet.

But it wasn't anyone from the hospital.

It was Gene.

'Rose? It's me.'

The seductive bass voice that never failed to raise gooseflesh on her skin made her instantly tingle. She hadn't yet taken off the diamond bracelet he'd sent and the glittering gems winked back at her as if daring her to remove it...

Dry-mouthed, she answered, 'What's up?'

She wanted to sound nonchalant, as if she didn't care that he should be ringing her so early in the morning, but as soon as she heard his voice her insides were deluged with a swarm of agitated butterflies.

'Tell me how you are this morning.'

'I'm—I'm fine...'

'I still wish that you'd come home with me.'

'I did the right thing. I was very tired. It's been an emotional time.'

'That's the reason why we shouldn't make any hasty decisions.'

Rose heard him take a deep breath in and remembered the comment he'd made about considering their feelings. It had knocked her for six. It certainly hadn't followed his infamous pattern of brief, 'take it or leave it' liaisons.

'I was worried that you might be upset about what happened yesterday and regret it,' he went on.

The comment made her burn as she recalled the sheer power of the elemental forces that had driven them to make love with such wild abandon in her boss's office. In the cold light of day it was hard to believe she'd behaved so recklessly.

'I'm not upset. We did what we did and I don't regret it. But, like I said…it's not going to happen again.'

She sucked in a breath and released it slowly in a bid to calm her nerves, but even as she'd said the words she'd been wishing she could take them back…

'By the way, thank you for the beautiful roses and the gift you sent.'

Frowning, she lifted her arm once again to examine the elegant diamond bracelet that adorned her wrist. The apricot silk dressing gown she was wearing, which she'd bought from a vintage clothing sale, couldn't help but complement the jewellery. The sensuous feel of the garment next to her skin made her feel like a million dollars.

Wearing both the bracelet *and* the gown, she felt like a whole other person…someone much more stylish and beautiful than the unremarkable woman she thought of herself as.

But her pleasure quickly died when she caught herself. She didn't want to give herself illusions of grandeur or to feel different or special just because she'd been given an expensive diamond bracelet. She wasn't like her mother, whose craving for the finer things in life had made her leave her loyal, dependable husband to be with a much wealthier man just because he could indulge her material desires…

'I'll keep the roses…but I'm afraid I won't be keeping the bracelet.'

There was a significant momentary silence at the other end of the phone. It was soon filled with an exasperated, 'Why not? I know how much you admire beautiful things and I wanted to give you something beautiful—so what's the problem?'

'It's a *diamond bracelet*, Gene. That's the problem. The clarity, cut and carat of the stones is amazing, so it's by no means a simple gift. Do you think that men give women gifts like that every day? They might in your exalted world, but they most definitely don't in mine. And it—it makes it hard for me to trust your motives. My ex used to give me pretty gifts when he was seeing other women behind my back and wanted to divert me from finding out. I know we're not serious, but if that's what *you're* going to do, Gene, then I'll save you wasting your time and your money by giving you the bracelet back. At least then we know where we stand.'

By the time she came to the end of her impassioned speech Rose could just imagine Gene dismissing it with a shrug of his impressive shoulders…more than likely encased in his usual impeccable tailoring. It was hard not to break down and cry… He might have talked about having feelings, but that didn't mean he'd honestly meant it.

'It sounds to me as if what happened yesterday *did* upset you, Rose. Why don't you have lunch with me today and we can talk?'

'About what a colossal mistake we made?' Even as she made the comment the churning emotion in her gut made a liar of her.

'You really believe that? A mistake suggests we had a choice in the matter and had time to think it through. If you recall, Rose, *thinking* didn't come into it. We were drawn together by an overpowering force of nature that we couldn't resist.'

And she had the sore spots on her body to prove it...

Feeling her face flame red, she replied, 'Anyway, I can't meet you for lunch. I have far too much work to do.'

'Do I have to keep reminding you that you're working for me now? You can have the whole damn day off if you want to.'

'But I don't *want* the day off.'

He made another exasperated sound and Rose was glad he couldn't see the tears that welled in her eyes.

'Meet me for lunch and let that be an end to it,' he ground out. 'I'll give you the name of the restaurant and you can meet me there. I'll pay for a cab.'

She sniffed and wiped her eyes, then stared blankly at the shimmering diamond bracelet that had slid down her slender-boned wrist to rest elegantly against her hand. 'I can pay for my own cab.'

'I might have guessed that you'd say that. Did I tell

you that I think you're the most stubborn woman I've ever met?'

It was Rose's turn to shrug. 'More than once... But it probably does you good to not have your own way all the time.'

Gene chuckled, and the sound elicited a burst of warmth inside her that made her want to count the minutes—no...the *seconds* until she could be with him again...

As Rose followed the smart, straight-backed *maître d'* to the table Gene had reserved she was sure that every single diner in the exclusive little restaurant watched her progress. As soon as she'd mentioned what seemed to be the magic words 'Eugene Bonnaire' she would have sworn that every one of the stylishly dressed customers seated at the tables had turned to see who was enquiring.

The table was in an intimately cordoned off alcove, tucked away at the back of the restaurant, and Rose's heart clanged hard as Gene stood up to greet her. He was wearing a slim-fitting charcoal suit, and the single-breasted jacket hung open to reveal a navy shirt and an azure silk tie. But it wasn't the colour of his shirt or tie that transfixed her. It was the arresting glint in his incredible blue eyes...

Every single muscle in her body stiffened and contracted at the undeniably voracious glance he gave her—because he was shamelessly undressing her with his eyes. That intense examining glance left her with nowhere to go...nowhere to run and hide...

He huskily murmured, 'Hi…' but she couldn't seem to find a single word with which to respond.

The discreet *maître d'* smiled, saying he would give them a few minutes to look at the menu. Then he politely left them alone.

Despite her see-sawing emotions Rose couldn't deny she'd been looking forward to their lunch date. That being the case, she'd decided to wear what was perhaps her most eye-catching outfit. She'd bared her shoulders in a top the colour of metallic silver, and had teamed it with a black chiffon mini-skirt with ebony tights and long leather boots.

She'd wanted Gene to see that she could look chic and classy and didn't need to dress in haute couture to prove it… Showcasing what she thought of as some of her best assets for their date—namely her tiny waist, slim arms and shapely legs—made her feel good.

In fact she was beginning to realise that she felt more womanly and attractive than she'd ever felt before when she was with him, and she wanted to let him see that—however their relationship *did* or *didn't* progress.

'You look sensational.'

His low-voiced compliment confirmed that she'd opted for the right outfit.

'I definitely heard an admiring gasp when you entered the restaurant. I'll bet everyone wants to know who you are.'

Although Gene's effusive compliments had stopped her in her tracks, confidently holding his gaze, Rose murmured, 'Thanks. You scrub up nicely yourself.'

With a gravel-voiced chuckle he moved round the

table to be closer to her. Then he made an elegant bow, like a gentleman from the upper echelons of society in one of those classic novels, and politely brushed the side of her cheek with a kiss.

Immediately the cool touch of his lips rendered Rose dangerously weak. *The reaction was definitely starting to become a habit.*

'Come and sit next to me…' he breathed, and it didn't once cross her mind to refuse. 'I haven't been able to stop thinking about you,' he confessed, his piercing cobalt eyes practically consuming her with their electric glance.

Rose set her handbag down on the chair next to her and twisted her hands together. 'I don't know whether that's a good or not so good thing. We're work colleagues now, remember?'

His sculpted lips shaped an amused grin, 'So our relationship is purely a working one, is it?'

'I didn't come here to talk about what's happened between us. I want to put that behind me and concentrate on doing a good job of selling off the antiques for you.'

'You can still do that…but it doesn't mean that we can't see each other outside of work.'

'Where are you going with this, Gene? I've already told you that I'd prefer it if we kept our association a professional one. Like I said before, I'm not interested in becoming one of your short-term little liaisons. In spite of what's happened, my decision hasn't changed.'

Gene sighed. As he pushed back his hair the eye-catching gold watch he wore glinted against his wrist. The bracelet was made unusually of rose gold, as was the intricate dial, set in relief against an ebony back-drop. Surely only the most confident and assured of men would be able to wear such a watch? And not only that, but wear it with enviable panache.

Rose didn't need to see the maker's name to know that it had been made by one of the most esteemed watch designers in the world. Her stomach lurched as it was brought home to her yet again just who Gene was and what he represented...

'I don't see our liaison as being a short-term one,' he told her, his tone etched with frustration. 'In fact I want us to have a *proper* relationship.'

Reaching for the water jug on the table, Rose poured a glass and gratefully swallowed some. She was almost lightheaded with shock. 'That's impossible. I know you don't do "proper" relationships, so why would you make an exception for me?'

His expression was serious. 'Why? Because I'm tired of denying the fact that I want something more, that's why. I'm tired of isolating myself from people. I haven't seen my family for months now, and it's near killing me.'

'Why haven't you seen them?'

'Because I'm too busy working.' Looking agonised, he shook his head. 'And because all I seem to do is hurt them when we're together.'

Rose caught his hand and held it. The heartfelt con-fession had utterly shaken her.

'Whatever has happened between you, there's always a way to make things better.'

'Maybe there is in your world, Rose...but not in mine.'

'Have you even talked to them about your belief that all you do is hurt them? That might not be the case at all. What if they're just waiting for you to come and talk things over?'

He glanced down at her slim hand, covering his, and his faint smile of acknowledgement twisted her heart.

'Maybe they are. I just haven't considered it.'

'Then you shouldn't waste any more time in going to see them and reconciling...that's my advice.'

'See how good you are for me? *That's* why it doesn't make sense for our relationship to be purely platonic.'

Rose sighed and carefully withdrew her hand. Again the fear arose that she was lulling herself into a false sense of security. 'Yes, it does. Just look at the facts. We're oceans apart, Gene. It doesn't matter how attracted we are to each other physically. The fact is we inhabit very different worlds. An association like ours is never going to work unless we keep things purely platonic.'

'You must be joking!' His lips twisted grimly. 'You might not want to admit I'm right, but our relationship is never, *ever* going to stay platonic. That would be like touching a lit match to some dry tinder and expecting it not to catch fire. Because that's what you do to me, Rose...you make me catch fire.'

Even as he finished speaking she knew he was going to kiss her. And what was more worrying was that she knew she wasn't going to try and stop him...

CHAPTER TEN

AS GENE'S MOUTH claimed Rose's in a hotly voracious kiss the depth and power of his desire genuinely scared him. It scared him to want and need a woman this much because it gave her a power over him that he wouldn't be able to repudiate easily. It wasn't just about the intense attraction he felt towards her either. The realisation that he might want something deeper was territory he'd never encountered before, and potentially it made him dangerously vulnerable.

But he simply couldn't leave her alone.

It would be like depriving himself of life-giving oxygen not to see her.

As his silken tongue danced with hers he heard her moan softly with pleasure and he gathered her into his arms. The sensation of her shapely and slender body pressed close into his chest inevitably made him tighten. *Why hadn't he suggested she met him at his apartment instead of at the restaurant?* At least then they could have tumbled into bed and continued what they'd started on the island and yesterday…

Intimately possessing Rose in the office might have

been the most red-hot sex he'd ever experienced, but it had fanned the flames of Gene's desire even more—despite his not using protection and the potential consequences.

But he didn't want to raise the topic of the morning-after pill right now...

Lifting his head, he glanced down into his lover's prettily flushed face and smiled. '*Now* do you believe me when I say a platonic relationship hasn't got a chance in hell of working? Not between you and me, Rose.'

Even though her beautiful eyes were drowsy with need, they also reflected unease. This was confirmed when she immediately extricated herself from Gene's embrace and moved further down in her seat.

'Well, we'd better not have *any* kind of relationship, then. We shouldn't have been intimate. Sex just confuses things. It always leads to trouble of some kind.'

Her words reminded him that Rose had been badly let down by an ex-boyfriend and that it wasn't just her mother running off with her rich lover that had made her so mistrustful of men...

'I told you that that's not going to happen between us. I may have played the field a little, but I've never lied to any woman about my intentions. That's why I've come clean with you and told you frankly what I've been feeling. I'm not like your ex-boyfriend and I won't let you down like he did. Can't you trust the connection we have and just be open to seeing where it goes?'

She glanced away for a second. 'I could... But it's

difficult when my ex had many of the same traits you have. I don't need to go into details—all you need to know is that he put work and ambition before everything else and basically did what he liked, because he thought it was some kind of inalienable right. Our relationship came very low down on his list of priorities, and if I dared complain he'd tell me he was only working as hard as he was for *me*. Then, finally, I found out that he'd regularly been cheating on me. I felt like such a fool. That's why I can't trust my feelings—and I can't trust men like *you*, Gene.'

'Just because he had similar traits to me and hurt you, Rose, it doesn't mean I'm going to behave in the same way. The least you can do is to give me a chance to prove myself.'

'It's a risk I can't afford to take, Gene. In any case the point is that I need to focus my attention on getting a new job, and you need to...you need to—'

He might be hard, hot and frustrated, but Gene couldn't deny he wanted to hear what she had to say. Raising an eyebrow, he murmured, 'Go on. What exactly *do* I need to do, Rose?'

'Forget it. What do I know? We lead very different lives.'

'You obviously have an opinion, so you may as well share it.'

Trapped, she heaved an annoyed sigh. 'Okay...but you're not going to like it. It's never going to work out between us, whatever our relationship. The way you live your life is totally alien to me, and I think it would

do you good to check in with the *real* world from time
to time.'

Gene suddenly sensed that he wasn't going to enjoy
hearing what else she had to say, but still he invited,
'Go on...'

'Well...you have a reputation for being able to get
anything you want, and you like the power that it gives
you. I sensed that the very first time I met you. There
was beauty all around you but you barely even saw it.
What you saw was a desirable property that you were
desperate to acquire and you would do anything to get
it. But let me ask you this: Don't you have enough property already? You probably don't even register what you
own because you're always looking for more. It must be
hard for the people who care about you because your
focus can't ever be on nurturing those relationships—
not if you're always so dissatisfied with what you've
got. You've told me yourself that you haven't seen your
parents in months, and I can see how much that hurts
you. Perhaps you ought to try and heal that relationship first, before you think about having one yourself.
In truth, I genuinely feel sorry for you—because I can
see that your wealth has stopped you from seeing the
things in life that really matter.'

Gene had never before been stunned into silence
but he was now. Rose's impassioned words hadn't just
unsettled him—they'd honestly disturbed him. He felt
as if he'd been put under a magnifying glass in the hot
sun. He was in pain and he was *furious*...

Reining in his temper, he countered, 'What do you
mean I should get in touch with the "real" world? Do

you think I was born with a silver spoon in my mouth and have no notion of what it's like to have to work hard for my living? My parents were immigrants and they both came from poverty-stricken backgrounds. They came over here, worked hard at various restaurants, then started up their own restaurant with minimal money and no help from anyone but each other. When I was old enough I started to help them and they taught me how to cook. When I realised I was good at it I discovered what I wanted to do in life and was determined to be a success. I've spent my life working hard to make my dreams into a reality...that's why my family and I will never be poor again. Do you think I'm going to apologise for that? Like *hell* I am!'

Rose's smooth brow puckered. 'It's commendable that you made your dreams come true, and of course I don't expect you to apologise for what you've achieved. I'm sure your parents must be very proud of you. But all I'm asking is haven't you ever thought about appreciating some of the more valuable things in life that are actually *free*?'

Gene glared irritably. 'Like what, for instance? It's been my experience that nothing is free. Fortunately I've always understood that the name of the game is money.'

'What about the ability to nurture and enjoy good relationships and—and to experience love? Do you think you have to pay for those too?'

He scowled. 'Love is a fool's game. It's too easy to lose. I prefer things that are more tangible.'

The look on Rose's face instantly conveyed her dismay, and Gene knew he would come to regret his cynical response.

'So that means that you would never risk loving someone?'

'Let me ask *you* a question, Rose. Is your mother a pretty woman? I'll bet she is. Your rich stepfather probably saw her as another desirable possession and she saw him as a better bet to take care of her than your dad because he was wealthy. Love doesn't have anything to do with it. You probably despise the man, but there was a mutually satisfying pay-off in that they both got exactly what they wanted.'

Stung, Rose shot up and grabbed her handbag. 'I don't despise him. I hate the fact that he used his wealth and fancy lifestyle to persuade my mum away from my dad. Yes, I know she wasn't entirely innocent. But I'll never admire *anyone* who uses their wealth in such a devious way—not even caring that they helped break a man's heart.'

Clutching the neat black leather bag she'd brought with her tightly against her chest, she used it as if it was a shield.

'Anyway, you can think what you like. You barely know me…much less my family.'

Rising to his feet, Gene folded his arms. 'You're right. But how can I *get* to know you when you don't trust people enough to let them get close? Going by what you said about your ex, it's clear that you have no intention of ever trusting that I might act honourably towards you.'

Her crimson-painted lips quivered and she looked

as if she was about to burst into tears. As much as he wanted to comfort her and take her in his arms, he elected not to.

This time her comments hadn't just touched a nerve—they had genuinely wounded him. It had stung to hear her suggest that his desire to keep on acquiring things must end up separating him from the people who cared about him... It stung because he knew it was *true*. It made him reflect uncomfortably on what he had done to his parents—on how his quest for 'more' and 'better' had indisputably hurt them and forged a chasm between them that was growing ever harder to bridge...

'I don't think I should stay for lunch after all,' she murmured.

'Why not...? I never had you down as a coward.'

Lifting her head, Rose stared. 'I'm not. I just think it's a case of wrong place, wrong time for us—and what's the point in us both being unhappy?'

Unable to make sense of anything much right then, Gene answered. 'I agree. There clearly isn't any point.'

'Anyway, there's one more thing before I go...'

Even as he fought to gain control of his pain and disappointment that she was leaving and, yes, the undeniable sense of loss that had engendered, he stayed grimly silent as Rose drew out the red velvet gift box from her handbag and laid it down on the table.

'I'm sure you meant well, but I can't accept this,' she said softly.

Then, with her pretty violet eyes glistening, she turned and walked out...

* * *

By the time Rose got to the hospital to see Philip it was already late and there was just half an hour left of visiting time. As she approached the bed and saw him intently perusing an antiques catalogue it hardly signified that he was looking so much better, because her heart was painfully leaden at the way she'd left Gene at the restaurant.

She'd told him some unpalatable truths and he would have had to be made out of stone not to be affected by it. She hadn't meant to be cruel. But neither had she wanted to lead him astray and let him believe she was happy to have a meaningless fling with him. Her feelings for Gene were far from meaningless.

That was why she'd returned the bracelet. It might be his habit to buy women expensive gifts in payment for sharing intimacy, but Rose knew she would never take anything from him that wasn't given freely or because it was important to him. If they had a real relationship it wouldn't be one that he had to *buy*...

'Rose...how lovely to see you!' Philip couldn't hide his delight when he saw her.

She bent down to kiss him. 'You too. I'm sorry I didn't get here earlier but I lost track of the time. I've been canvassing as many dealers as I can to get them to buy the rest of the antiques. I did quite well this afternoon, I'm happy to report, so all the time and effort was worth it.'

When she pulled out the grey utilitarian chair next to the bed and tiredly dropped down into it her smile wasn't as animated as she would have wished. But, quickly gathering herself, Rose delved into her bag for the generous carton of plump red grapes that she'd brought.

'I know you'd probably prefer some of your favourite Belgian chocolate, but I thought I'd better not lead you astray.'

'Why on earth not…? Even an old fogey like me can use a little of what they fancy from time to time, can't they?'

'Well…perhaps next time I'll smuggle some in. How are you? Any news on those other tests you had?'

The time seemed to pass in a flash, and most of the other patients' visitors had left when Rose finally plucked up the courage to share what was uppermost in her mind…*Gene*.

'Philip?' Nervously smoothing her hand across the crisp white hospital counterpane, she leant towards him. 'Can I talk to you about something? It's a personal matter.'

'Of course you can, my dear. Is it to do with the shop? Are you perhaps finding it too much of a struggle to sell off the antiques as well as dealing with everything else that needs doing before Bonnaire comes in and takes over?'

Even the mention of Gene's surname had the power to make Rose ache with longing. She couldn't help wondering if she would ever see him again after their heated exchange at the restaurant. What if he sent his secretary or some minion to oversee things at the antiques store, just so he wouldn't have to come face to face with her?

It was like a dagger in her heart to think that he might so quickly forget the staggeringly powerful passion that had driven them to make love in Philip's office and treat it as though it was nothing important. Look at the risk they'd taken.

But the declaration he'd made at the restaurant that he wouldn't risk loving someone—that love was 'a fool's game'—couldn't help but fill her with more sorrow. If Rose had privately nursed an impossible hope that somehow he *could* learn to love her, his searing admission had obliterated it.

'I'm fine organising the sale of the antiques and everything else. That's not what I wanted to talk to you about. It's much more personal than that.'

Not commenting, Philip leant back against his plumped-up pillows and waited patiently for her to continue. Meeting his infinitely kind gaze, Rose assured herself that it would be all right—that he would understand and wouldn't judge her…

'I—I've fallen for someone…' she told him, even as her privately anguished feelings threatened to overwhelm her.

'Are you telling me that you're in love, Rose?'

Nodding miserably, she sensed her lip quiver.

Philip smiled. He couldn't have looked happier. 'But that's *wonderful* news. Who's the lucky man?'

'You don't need to know his name… I—I'd rather keep that private for now, if you don't mind. All I can tell you is that he's someone completely unsuitable.'

'But that hasn't stopped you from having feelings for

him?' he observed gently. Her comment clearly hadn't fazed him.

His reaction genuinely surprised her. 'No, it hasn't. But he's the absolute antithesis of me,' she insisted. 'It's hit me like a ton of bricks that I should feel this way about him.'

Philip was thoughtful. 'Falling in love can happen in a myriad different ways, Rose. For some it's a slow progression as they get to know each other…with others their eyes can literally meet across a room and they know instantly that he or she is the person they want to spend the rest of their life with. For others still it can knock them flat when they're simply going about their business, convinced that everything is under control and that nothing can possibly make them deviate from the path they're set on. It sounds to me, Rose, as if you fall into that category.'

'It's true. I never even *wanted* to fall in love. I schooled myself against it…especially after Joe cheated on me. Do you remember? But now that it's happened it's threatening everything I believe in. Doing what's right, I mean—the tenets that my dad taught me and stood by. Loving this man *isn't* doing what's right. I feel so guilty and I'm ashamed that I've let everyone down.'

Philip frowned. 'Everyone? Who do you imagine you've let down, Rose?'

Twisting her fingers restlessly together, she sighed. 'I've let *you* down, Philip. You've done so much for me and you deserve better'

'My dear…'

She found her agitated hands captured in his frail ones and subdued.

'You're behaving as though you've committed some heinous crime. Since when has falling in love been a criminal offence? Your feelings are no concern of anyone else's. Yes, the people who love you only want the best for you—but how does anybody know what's best for someone else? It's surely better to risk all for love than to turn away from it because of your fear of letting people down and living a life filled with regret and "if only".'

More than a little shocked, she stared. 'You sound as if you know exactly what that's like. Have you ever loved someone you turned away from because of what other people thought?'

The distinguished man nodded slowly, and his pale blue eyes couldn't hide the sadness that his memories must have aroused. 'I didn't just turn away from the lady because of what people thought, Rose... I turned away from her because I chose to focus on my career rather than go with her into the unknown. She was an artist...a rather wonderful one. She was ten years younger than me and she wanted to travel the world and be inspired by the vistas she saw to do her painting. She had no time for what she called "the safe option"—having a career, marrying someone and living what she used to call "a conventionally stultifying life of suburban boredom". She was a free spirit.'

He coughed a little and glanced away for a moment—but not before Rose spied the glint of moisture in his eyes.

'Her name was Elizabeth and I loved her more than life itself.'

'Do you mind if I ask…is that the reason why you've never married?'

Nodding again, he released her hands. 'There was never anyone for me but *her*. I could never even contemplate it. That's why you must follow your heart, Rose. There's no need for guilt and shame. Don't be like me and live a life of regret, imagining what might have been. I'm sure if your father was still here he would tell you the same.'

'And what about Elizabeth…? Did you ever see her again?'

'Sadly not… She said she thought it best that we didn't stay in touch. I just pray that wherever she is she continues to enjoy her travels and paint her pictures. It makes me happy to think of her doing what she loves.'

Leaning towards the bed, Rose affectionately brushed the side of his weathered cheek with her lips. 'Bless you, Philip. What you've just told me means more than I can say. I feel as though a great burden has been lifted from me. I feel lighter and—and more hopeful that whatever happens it will all work out. Although I'm still scared the man concerned might not feel the same…'

'I don't think you need have any fear about that.'

'Thanks. You're good for a girl's ego—you know that?'

Glancing towards the door, she noticed there was a stern-looking nurse pointing up at the wall clock to indicate that visiting hours were over.

Turning her gaze back to her boss, she said, 'I'd better go. I'll keep in touch by phone as often as I can, and let you know how I'm getting on with selling the antiques. And if there's anything you want me to put by for you, I will. One more thing: please let me know if you get a date for when you can come home, won't you?'

'Of course I will. Now, go and see your mysterious man. Maybe one day soon you'll feel able to tell me his name? In the meantime, tell him from me that the gods of good fortune smiled on him the day he set eyes on you, Rose.'

The first thing Gene saw when he opened his eyes the next morning was the red velvet jewel box. On his return from the restaurant he'd dropped it onto his dressing table as though he despised it.

Did Rose have any idea how much she'd humiliated him with her vehement little diatribe about the way he lived? And—more to the point—the way she'd all but thrown his gift back in his face? Hadn't the message he'd written meant anything to her? He was sick to his stomach that she'd scorned him.

Because he'd been so agitated, and hadn't been able to face returning to his office, he'd gone straight to his apartment and started to work from home. Deliberately focusing on his plans for the new restaurant, he'd sought to distract himself from thoughts of Rose by contacting as many of the professionals he'd previously courted who worked in the high-end hospitality business to remind them about the new Thames-side restaurant he was planning.

As Gene had confidently expected, there was plenty

of interest about coming to work for him and he'd been able to get quite a few people to commit.

After imbibing a couple of glasses of the rare Bordeaux he'd brought over from his cellar in Paris, he had talked and planned and made arrangements into the early hours. And finally, when sheer exhaustion had got the better of him, he'd kicked off his shoes, pulled off his tie and fallen into bed fully clothed.

But even as his burning eyes had drifted closed Gene hadn't been able to banish the memory of Rose's beautiful face, her mesmerising violet gaze, and the realisation had hit him that for the very first time in his life he was madly, head over heels in love.

The knowledge should have filled him with joy—but not when the sobering thought that the object of his affections was a woman who neither wanted nor regarded him had quickly followed it...

He had been utterly despondent. And that was why this morning, when he saw the red velvet box containing the diamond bracelet, he was painfully reminded that Rose had given it back to him without a qualm. She wasn't remotely impressed by his wealth or his ability to acquire whatever he wanted. In fact she definitely saw it as a negative rather than a desirable attribute.

She was refreshingly different from any of the women who moved in his so-called 'elite' circle. She wanted nothing of him other than that he start to look around and see the things in life that were important— the things that came in abundance just by dint of being born human...the things that came without a price tag, like nature and beauty and the possibility of being close to someone special…

Nothing that Gene could buy her or give her was ever going to convince Rose that underneath all his wealth and acquisitions had once been a genuinely good man who had somehow taken a wrong turn.

His understandable drive to make money and help secure his parents' future and his own after losing his sister had become insatiable… He'd started out doing it for all the right reasons, but the desire had long since become an addiction. He knew no peace and had no decent relationships to speak of. *All he did was work.* It took far more energy than people realised to maintain a position like his, and that was why he'd had no time to build relationships.

He'd had his sanctuary built in the hope that as well as not having to contend with the day-to-day bombardment of the press there, the isolation might one day help him deal properly with his grief so he could start to heal the out-of-control compulsion for 'more' that plagued him.

If only he had the courage to confide in Rose and explain *why* he had become so addicted. Gene would tell her that he'd thought it would protect him from the spectre of loss that haunted him… He would tell her about his sister and how she'd died unexpectedly and cruelly when she was just three years old. She had been the family's 'bright star' and they would never forget her…

Dropping his head into his hands, he thought hard. The only solution that would restore any hope for him was if he came up with a realistic plan to win Rose back—because suddenly the idea of living without her was too unbearable to contemplate…

CHAPTER ELEVEN

ROSE HAD RESISTED making her all-important call to Gene's office until she'd finished work, telling herself that he would no doubt be working late himself. Yet the truth that lurked beneath her delay taunted her, and all that day her insides were tied in painful knots because of it. She was terrified that he might not want to talk to her…that after she'd walked out on him at the restaurant he had mulled things over and decided he just didn't need the grief of a woman who perpetually liked to speak her mind.

When she finally picked up the phone and rang him she'd worked herself up into such a state that she felt physically sick.

'Mr Bonnaire is not in the office today,' his snooty secretary informed her, her imperious tone suggesting that a nonentity like Rose was wasting her time.

Immediately that put Rose's back up.

'Well, if he's not in the office can you tell me where I can reach him? He's not answering his mobile.'

'No. I'm afraid I can't.'

'But this is important!'

The woman expelled an irritated sigh. 'If Mr Bonnaire had wanted you to reach him he would have left instructions, Miss Heathcote. All I can tell you is that he doesn't want to be disturbed by *anyone* today.'

'But—'

'Goodbye, Miss Heathcote.'

The receiver was firmly put down to signal the end of the call and now Rose really *was* worried. The thought that she'd lost her chance to make amends with Gene was agonising. Why had she left it so late to ring him? What if he was out of the country on business somewhere and wasn't going to be back for days—or maybe even *weeks*?

Unable to sit still, she found herself restlessly making tea in the kitchen as she thought hard about what to do. She was taking her first sip of the hot beverage when the answer came to her. She knew *exactly* what she had to do...

The idea so excited her that she felt dizzy. Gripped by a steely determination and a newfound daring that she hadn't known she had in her, she emptied the mug of tea, grabbed her coat and bag and turned out the lights. Then, locking the doors of the antiques shop behind her, she hailed a cab to take her to the station...

Nearly drowned by the sea spray on the turbulent crossing, Rose smoothed back her plastered hair and turned up the collar on her raincoat with damp, icy fingers. Any conversation with Rory the boatman was impossible above the eldritch mourning of the wind and with the craft's constant leaping over the waves and its roll-ercoaster dive back down into them.

The young man had warned her when she'd boarded. ''Tis a rough crossing you'll face today, Rose. Sure you want to risk it?'

With her heart thudding fit to burst, she'd answered, 'If you're willing to risk it, then so am I. But I don't want you to cross if you honestly feel it's too dangerous.'

In answer to that statement Rory had grinned and said, 'I've crossed in worse seas than this and lived to tell the tale. But the message you're taking to His Lordship must be powerful important if you're willing to risk life and limb to take it to him, Rose. Did you let him know you were coming?'

So her instincts about Gene going to the island had been right.

She'd breathed out a relieved sigh and climbed into the boat. 'No…I didn't. Let's just say I want to surprise him.'

'Doesn't strike me as a man who likes surprises much…but I'm sure he'll make an exception for this one. He's a good man—in spite of all the rubbish the press say about him.'

True to his word, the boatman delivered Rose safely to the island. He even insisted on waiting for her to start negotiating the climb up the hill towards the house before leaving, calling out that he would bring the boat back one more time that afternoon 'just in case'.

Although she was chilled to the bone, and her damp clothing was clinging wetly to her body as she climbed the rocky incline, Rose hardly registered the discomfort. She was too tense to worry about it. But as she approached the futuristic dwelling that loomed out of the landscape the strangest sense of coming home washed over her, and she hugged the feeling to her as if it was something infinitely precious.

Glancing down at herself, she couldn't deny she wished she looked better. But then what did that signify, as long as Gene was pleased she'd made the journey? Because if he wasn't…

'Don't even *think* it…' she muttered crossly.

Remembering where to locate the dwelling's entrance, she moved her hand over the sensor and to her profound relief the curved doors slid opened. As she stepped onto the flawless parquet floor she heard the doors swish closed behind her. Swallowing hard, she nervously smoothed her hand down her damp raincoat. How was she going to let Gene know that she was there? Should she call out? Or simply just go and find him?

Still unsure, she kicked off her shoes, firmed the strap of her bag more securely over her shoulder and set off towards the living room. Even as she walked she detected the warm and tantalising scent of the Frenchman's cologne, and the provocative trail made her feel weak with excitement and longing.

'Well, well, well. Look who the wind's blown in.'

The tall, broad-shouldered Adonis with golden lights in his otherwise dark hair was staring out at the crashing waves through the panoramic windows. He turned slowly. There wasn't even the briefest acknowledgement of surprise in his piercing blue eyes. *It was just as though he'd been expecting her.*

Rose felt the strap of her bag slide off her shoulder and didn't move to stop it from falling to the floor. 'You said—you said that to me once before,' she answered, her teeth helplessly chattering.

'Did I?' Moving towards her, Gene smiled. 'I can see I'm going to have to find a new repertoire.'

'You don't look a bit surprised. How did you know that I would come here to look for you?'

'There are some things that are hard to explain…particularly when it comes to feelings. But that will have to keep for later. More importantly, you need to get out of those wet clothes and into a hot shower right now.'

Rose wasn't going to deny it. 'Yes, I do… But what about you, Gene? What do *you* need?'

His blue eyes mirrored his surprise…his pleasure too. 'What I need, sweetheart, is to join you,' he said huskily. 'You okay with that?'

Transfixed, Rose silently conveyed her agreement.

He stepped closer and his strong, muscular arm confidently encircled her waist. Feeling as though she was in a dream, it was as though her feet didn't even touch the floor as she let him lead her into the corridor and straight to his private suite.

In the state-of-the-art bathroom with a mosaic tiled floor in dazzling azure and wall-to-wall mirrors, Gene turned on the water in the spacious shower and soon the whole room was filled with hot, perfumed steam.

Even as she tried to take in what was happening the vehement desire that surged through her body easily took precedence over what was in her mind. When he came to her and helped dispense with her raincoat she was more than happy to let him.

After laying it on a nearby chair he came back to her, and his handsome face was a study of intense concentration as piece by piece he started to remove Rose's clothing. She was still shivering—but this time it wasn't from the cold.

'Together we make fire,' he'd told her once, and it was true.

Placing his big hands either side of her hips, he expertly removed her skimpy underwear, and she felt every touch and stroke of his flesh as though she couldn't bear to be without it.

Then he drew her towards him and, gravel-voiced, commanded, 'Kiss me.'

Rose had no intention of denying him and hungrily complied. Their mouths opened helplessly as soon as their lips collided and they were reunited with the molten heat that seemed to be generated so effortlessly whenever they were together. Now that heat intensified and burst into full scorching flame, and as their kisses became ever more urgent, with Gene's deliciously velvet mouth all but devouring her, Rose's hands started to tear desperately at his clothes.

When he was naked, for the very first time she had a true 'up close and personal' look at his magnificent body. As well as being muscular, fit and toned, he was heavily aroused, primed to take her, and she could hardly wait until the moment when they would join together...

Feeling deliriously weak and hungry, she wrapped

her arms round his neck and begged softly, 'Take me into the shower...*please*...'

Lifting her against him effortlessly, so that her slim thighs clamped tightly round his lean waist, Gene stooped down to his discarded jeans and extracted a strip of slim foil packets. When he stood again, with his indomitable brow furrowing, she noticed his smile was a little self-conscious.

'I don't want to put you in the same position I put you in last time and have you worrying about getting pregnant,' he confessed.

'Would you be shocked if I admitted that I actually thought about *not* taking that morning-after pill?' Rose asked him softly.

'Why? Why would you do that?'

'Perhaps we'd better talk about that later...' She smiled.

Gene immediately concurred. 'All I want you to think about now is the sweet, unadulterated pleasure I'm going to give you, sweetheart.'

Bending his head, he stole another incendiary, open-mouthed kiss and Rose's body all but melted as he carried her into the hot, steamy shower.

The first time he took her hard and fast, and she gasped her need and pleasure out loud as hot rivulets of water deluged their naked bodies. They ran down her hair and face and streamed over her breasts as Gene claimed her again and again, and finally Rose couldn't hold back the elemental force that threatened to take her over the edge any longer... *In his arms she came undone.*

Rapturous with the hot tide of sensual feeling that overwhelmed her, she felt tears of joy flood into her eyes and mingle with the water from the shower. Her lover released a deep guttural groan and grew still as he climaxed.

For a while both of them couldn't speak. Then he looked down at her and carefully eased her back onto her feet. Even in the steam that enveloped them she saw his blue eyes shine as she'd never seen them shine before…

'We've been together for half an hour at least, angel, and I haven't yet told you how beautiful you are.'

Sighing with satisfaction, he pulled her against him and covered her eyelids, nose and mouth with infinitely tender kisses that made Rose catch her breath and stare at him in wonder.

'I promise I'm going to make up for that, sweetheart—starting now, by telling you that you're one gorgeous, sexy woman. I don't know what I did to bring you to me—only that I'm *beyond* grateful that you're here.'

Rose's smile was warm and loving as she stroked a strand of glistening wet hair back from his lightly ridged forehead. Her heart was so full it was hard to put her feelings into words.

'I couldn't have stayed away, Gene. Did you think I *could*?'

Shaking his head, he captured her hand. 'When you left me in the restaurant after saying those things about the way I conducted myself… I won't lie to you and tell you that I didn't resent it—because I *did*.' He paused to lift her hand to his lips and kissed it. 'But I knew I was angry because you were the one person who had dared to tell me the truth.'

'I didn't mean to hurt you.'

'I know you didn't. But it had to be done, Rose. I was in a hell of my own making and you came along and set me free. Maybe now I have a chance to redeem myself?'

'Let's dry each other off and go to bed, shall we? I want to hold you in my arms and tell you exactly what I feel about you, Eugene Bonnaire…businessman *extraordinaire.*'

Her smile was teasing and unashamedly seductive, and she revelled in the new sensation of feminine power that she'd discovered—no holds barred.

The second time he took her Gene deliberately slowed things down. In the lavish double bed, with its satin and silk sheets, he took his time and savoured every incredible, joyous moment of making love with Rose. She was the most giving woman in every respect, and she took just as much delight and pleasure in exploring him as he did her.

Her sweetly shaped breasts, slim hips and silkily smooth thighs perfectly complemented his hard, lean physique when he took her in his arms and caressed her. And when he gazed at the stunning revelation of her bare body lying on his silk sheets he saw that she was the perfect 'pocket Venus'.

He found it hard to understand how he had ever thought any other woman beautiful. How could he have when there had always been one vitally important missing ingredient? The heart-to-heart connection that now made him hopeful and helped him look forward to a truly *joyous* future instead of one that he'd feared would bring only more sorrow.

Rose was lying atop him and had been teasingly nipping at the soft flesh of his lower lip. As much as he was enjoying it, in one deft motion Gene had manoeuvred her to lie next to him. Turning towards her, he cupped her small jaw in his big hand and for a long moment was lost in the beauty of her radiant violet gaze.

'You said it crossed your mind not to take that morning-after pill. Will you tell me why?'

Rose didn't shy away from meeting the intensity she saw in his glance and said, 'I couldn't help wondering what a child we made would look like. And for the first time in my life I realised I wanted children. I wanted a family of my own.'

'Do you still feel like that?'

'If the right man came along I wouldn't hesitate.'

Trying not to give way to a delighted grin, Gene eased out a long slow breath. 'And has he?'

'What do *you* think?'

He answered her, leaving her in no doubt, with a lingering hot kiss.

When they both came up for air he asked, 'Out of interest, how did you know I would be here on the island?' His breath hitched as he waited to hear her reply.

Rose sighed. 'How do you think? I *sensed* that you were here…that you would be waiting for me. I didn't even stop to pack. I just jumped in a cab. My only worry was that you wouldn't forgive me.'

'Forgive you for what?'

She grimaced. 'For taking it upon myself to tell you where you'd been going wrong, that's what. It's not like I'm some kind of expert. I've made plenty of mistakes too.'

Unable to resist teasing her, Gene made himself look serious. 'Oh? What kind of mistakes?'

'Funny enough, always trying to "do the right thing." Not allowing myself to really live...to trust that if I listened to my heart it wouldn't lead me astray. My dad found it hard to trust too. He was a wonderful man, but he could be unforgiving about making mistakes. And he was so afraid I was going to turn out like my mother if he didn't make certain rules about how I should behave. The thing is, she isn't a bad person—but he probably forgot all the reasons he'd once loved her when she left him and he was worried that one day I might replicate her behaviour.'

'You mean he was afraid you might run off with some unscrupulous billionaire who, after he'd seduced you, would make you fall in love with his wealthy and essentially empty lifestyle?'

Feeling the bitter bite of regret, Gene couldn't help his sardonic tone.

Immediately concerned, Rose put her hand on his shoulder and lightly stroked it. 'It's not your rich lifestyle that I fell in love with...it's the man I always sensed was beneath the aloof and polished façade. It's *you* that I love, Gene. You and no other.'

Somehow Gene's breath felt as if it was trapped inside his chest. His heart was racing so hard he could scarcely think straight. Then he realised that he was hearing the words he'd thought never to hear. Not in *this* life anyway…

'You *love* me?'

Rose looked perturbed. 'You sound as if you might doubt it?'

'It's not that I doubt you mean it, Rose. I'm just surprised…*delighted* and surprised. The truth is I don't think I'm a very lovable person. My own parents probably have trouble even *liking* me. Don't think I'm feeling sorry for myself—I can't help but be a realist.'

'I don't believe that your parents don't like you. And I certainly don't believe they don't *love* you. A parent's love is unconditional, isn't it?'

He shrugged. 'They tell me that they care, but it was my sister they adored.'

'You had a sister?'

'Yes…'

Instead of pushing the feelings of grief away, as he usually did, Gene let them come. He remembered the fierce joy he'd felt whenever he was with Francesca, and the sense that he would protect her with his life if he could. To his everlasting regret, he hadn't been able to.

Swallowing hard, he smiled painfully. 'Her name was Francesca. She died when she was just three, after a short and painful illness.'

Rose's hand stilled against his shoulder. 'Gene, I'm so sorry. How old were *you*?'

'I was nine.'

'Your poor family… You must have all been utterly devastated.'

'We were. We still are. That's why I was determined

to do everything I could to make sure my parents at least never had to worry about money. Unfortunately things didn't go exactly as I'd planned. My desire to secure their future got rather out of hand. I became addicted to the pleasure of seeing my bank balance grow larger and larger—and to the kudos of being successful… I thought it would protect me from the spectre of loss that had haunted me since losing Francesca. But I lost sight of my reasons. As you said to me at the restaurant, Rose…I just didn't know when enough was enough. And along the way, when I saw that my relationships—especially with women—weren't fulfilling, because they were mostly meaningless, I think I lost a little bit of my soul.'

'Oh, baby…'

She kissed him tenderly and it was then that Gene sensed the truth in her touch. His heart leapt.

'I love you too, Rose. The thought of not being with you for the rest of my life is torture.'

She wrapped her arms firmly around him and kissed him again. When she glanced up she was grinning. 'The last thing I want to do is torture you, my love. I want to spend the rest of my life making you happy. And I'll tell anyone who cares to listen what a good and kind man you are. The kind of man who always makes the people who love him proud.'

'On that subject: I'd like you to be with me when I go and talk to my parents, Rose. I want to tell them how I've been feeling, why I've grown more and more distant from them. I also want to share with them the way I felt after we lost Francesca. And lastly…'

'Tell me?'

'I want to tell them that I've met the woman of my dreams.'

Rose dimpled. 'Now you're going to make me cry...'

'There's something else I'd like you to do for me.'

'What's that?'

'I'd like you to take back the bracelet I gave you. I meant what I said on the note I sent with it. You *are* the hidden diamond that I didn't expect. If you accept my gift, and the heartfelt intention that it was given with, I'll know it means that you love me for the *real* Gene Bonnaire—not the ruthless businessman that the world sees, but the very fallible and ordinary man who doesn't mind admitting that he's made quite a few mistakes in his life. However...the one mistake I'll *never* make is to walk away from the woman who is far more precious and valuable to me than anything material I could ever acquire or achieve... The woman who I hope will one day be my wife and the mother of my children.'

Rose was crying...crying inconsolably.

All Gene could do was to hold her lovingly against him until she grew quiet, all the while telling her how much he loved and adored her.

Then he asked her to marry him.

When she looked up at him she answered, 'Yes! Of *course* I'll marry you!' And the happiness that shone from her beautiful violet eyes shimmered like the most exquisite diamond of all...even though they were drenched with tears...

EPILOGUE

ROSE HAD WANTED to make her afternoon visit to her husband's Parisian office a surprise. She'd agreed beforehand to meet him at a sumptuous and classy restaurant in the city, to have a late lunch with his parents and her mother and stepfather, but in the end she'd made the decision to meet him at his office first, so that they could travel to the restaurant together.

She wanted to pinch herself at the way things had changed. Not only had Gene been reunited with his family, but Rose had also started to rebuild her relationship with her mother. And, to top it all, just a few short weeks ago she and Gene had been married in the most exquisite Gothic church in Kensington. Even the presence of a flock of paparazzi hadn't spoiled the day. Unbelievably, she was now Mrs Bonnaire.

Walking down the richly carpeted corridor of what she teasingly referred to as 'the presidential suite', she felt her tummy deluged with butterflies. She couldn't help being nervous at the prospect of seeing the man she adored. Their passionate relationship had been nothing less than a dream come true. Every day when she woke up next to him Rose told Gene that he took her breath away.

Today she'd donned one of her prettiest dresses underneath a stylish designer jacket, and she was particularly hoping that he would notice.

'Mrs Bonnaire. How nice to see you. Is Mr Bonnaire expecting you?'

His new smartly attired middle-aged secretary, Martine, was genuinely pleased to see her, and had made no secret of the fact that she was pleased and delighted that her handsome boss had found the woman he declared to be 'the love of his life'.

Rose sent up a silent prayer that her husband wasn't with a colleague or a client. She was literally *aching* to see him.

'No, Martine. He's not expecting me. But if he's free can I just go in and see him?'

'But of course.'

After knocking briefly on the panelled oak door, she walked inside. Gene's office was not just stylish, it was bright and beautiful too. Rose loved the way that sunlight never seemed to fail to be pouring in from the large plate-glass windows that looked out onto the busy city whenever she visited.

Today was no different. As her avid gaze fell upon her husband she saw how the light reflected burnished lights in his immaculately cut dark hair.

He turned to welcome his visitor. 'I knew it had to be you, my love.' He smiled. 'I think I'm psychically attuned to that polite little knock of yours.'

Rose moved swiftly towards him for his embrace. 'I know I said I'd meet you at the restaurant, but—'

'Is something wrong?'

Seeing his worried frown, she hastened to assure him. 'No, there's nothing wrong. I just couldn't wait to see you. Do you mind?'

'You may as well ask me if I need to breathe.' Gene chuckled. 'Not only have you decided to surprise me with an impromptu visit, but you've worn that very pretty red dress that I love on you.'

He nuzzled the side of her neck and the heat he exuded along with the seductive scent of his cologne made Rose instantly weak.

'I'm just wondering if I should lock the door and lower the blinds. And if I have time to take it off you and make love to you before we go to the restaurant.'

'Ordinarily I'd agree it was a good idea, but we're meeting both your parents and mine for lunch—remember?' Her cheeks dimpled and she gently touched her palm to his cheek. 'And not just that—I have something I need to tell you before we leave.'

Lifting her hand away, her husband pressed his lips in a briefly tender kiss against hers. 'That sounds ominous…' he remarked teasingly.

'But only in a good way, I hope?'

'Depends what it is you're going to tell me.'

'I'm pregnant. We're going to have a baby, Gene!'

His blue eyes widened, glinting in the sunlight. 'This is true? I mean, you know this for sure, Rose?'

'I took a pregnancy test this morning and it came out positive.' Her heart was hammering as she spoke, but there was no need for anxiety. Already she could see the joy in his expression.

'*Mon Dieu*... I'm going to be a father! We are going to be parents. This is the most wonderful thing I've ever heard, my love!'

Gene caught her to him and passionately kissed her. When they came up for air he pushed a button at the side of his desk. The lock on the door firmly clicked shut and the cream-coloured blinds at the windows started to lower smoothly.

He turned back to Rose and gently divested her of her jacket, and then he expertly pulled down the zip at the side of her pretty red dress.

'I've decided we definitely have time to make love before we go to lunch...' He smiled. 'Our parents won't mind if we're late... Not when we tell them that they're going to be grandparents.'

Rose's eyes moistened as she gazed up at him. 'Have you *any* idea just how much I love you?' she breathed.

For an electrifying moment Gene looked serious. 'If it comes anywhere near to the depth and breadth of the love I have for you, Rose, then I know I must be the most blessed man on earth.'

* * * * *

Available July 21, 2015

#3353 CHATSFIELD'S ULTIMATE ACQUISITION

The Chatsfield

by Melanie Milburne

Isabelle Harrington is *furious* when arrogant playboy Spencer Chatsfield becomes her new boss. He's also the man who shattered her heart years ago. The only thing she can't stand more than Spencer is the sizzling chemistry *still* burning between them!

#3354 THE GREEK DEMANDS HIS HEIR

The Notorious Greeks

by Lynne Graham

Leo Zikos is pleased to have secured a perfectly *convenient* fiancée, until Grace Donovan's impeccable beauty tempts him to pursue one last night of freedom... But that night, and the positive pregnancy test that follows, blows Leo's plans apart!

#3355 HIS SICILIAN CINDERELLA

Playboys of Sicily

by Carol Marinelli

Matteo Santini bought one night with Bella Gatti to protect her innocence, but then she disappeared. Now, forced together at a wedding, he wants a reckoning. The only way Bella will be leaving the party is with Matteo—via his bed!

#3356 THE PERFECT CAZORLA WIFE

by Michelle Smart

Charley Cazorla strides back into her soon-to-be ex-husband's life with a plan. Except Raul has his own ideas! To save Charley's business, the Spaniard demands his own payment: she must resume her role as the *perfect* wife—in *every* sense!

HPCNM0715RA

#3357 THE SINNER'S MARRIAGE REDEMPTION
Seven Sexy Sins
by Annie West
Flynn Marshall is determined to rush stunning Ava Cavendish to the altar at the first opportunity. A trophy bride should complete his plans, but the desire Ava inflames in this untouchable CEO soon turns his ordered strategy on its head...

#3358 THE MARAKAIOS BABY
The Marakaios Brides
by Kate Hewitt
Margo Ferras knows that she must give up devishly seductive Leo Marakaios in order to protect her heart. But when she discovers that she's pregnant with his child, Margo walks back into Leo's life and asks *him* to marry *her*!

#3359 CAPTIVATED BY THE GREEK
by Julia James
Salesgirl Mel may not be Nikos Parakis's type, but she can't resist his tempting offer: a no-strings romance under the sizzling sun. But parting ways is made impossible when sultry nights with the captivating Greek leave Mel carrying his heir!

#3360 CLAIMED FOR HIS DUTY
Greek Tycoons Tamed
by Tara Pammi
Stavros Sporades agreed to marry heiress Leah Huntington to protect her, but now she's demanding a divorce! Stavros wants proof Leah's troubled past is behind her, but one night of desire reveals that she might have been innocent all along...

YOU CAN FIND MORE INFORMATION ON UPCOMING HARLEQUIN® TITLES, FREE EXCERPTS AND MORE AT WWW.HARLEQUIN.COM.

HPCNM0715RB

REQUEST YOUR
FREE BOOKS!

◆HARLEQUIN

Presents®

2 FREE NOVELS PLUS
2 FREE GIFTS!

YES! Please send me 2 FREE Harlequin Presents® novels and my 2 FREE gifts (gifts are worth about $10). After receiving them, if I don't wish to receive any more books, I can return the shipping statement marked "cancel." If I don't cancel, I will receive 6 brand-new novels every month and be billed just $4.30 per book in the U.S. or $5.24 per book in Canada. That's a saving of at least 13% off the cover price! It's quite a bargain! Shipping and handling is just 50¢ per book in the U.S. and 75¢ per book in Canada.* I understand that accepting the 2 free books and gifts places me under no obligation to buy anything. I can always return a shipment and cancel at any time. Even if I never buy another book, the two free books and gifts are mine to keep forever.

106/306 HDN GHRP

Name _____ (PLEASE PRINT) _____

Address _____ Apt. # _____

City _____ State/Prov. _____ Zip/Postal Code _____

Signature (if under 18, a parent or guardian must sign)

Mail to the **Reader Service:**
IN U.S.A.: P.O. Box 1867, Buffalo, NY 14240-1867
IN CANADA: P.O. Box 609, Fort Erie, Ontario L2A 5X3

**Are you a current subscriber to Harlequin Presents® books
and want to receive the larger-print edition?
Call 1-800-873-8635 or visit www.ReaderService.com.**

* Terms and prices subject to change without notice. Prices do not include applicable taxes. Sales tax applicable in N.Y. Canadian residents will be charged applicable taxes. Offer not valid in Quebec. This offer is limited to one order per household. Not valid for current subscribers to Harlequin Presents books. All orders subject to credit approval. Credit or debit balances in a customer's account(s) may be offset by any other outstanding balance owed by or to the customer. Please allow 4 to 6 weeks for delivery. Offer available while quantities last.

Your Privacy—The Reader Service is committed to protecting your privacy. Our Privacy Policy is available online at www.ReaderService.com or upon request from the Reader Service.

We make a portion of our mailing list available to reputable third parties that offer products we believe may interest you. If you prefer that we not exchange your name with third parties, or if you wish to clarify or modify your communication preferences, please visit us at www.ReaderService.com/consumerchoice or write to us at Reader Service Preference Service, P.O. Box 9062, Buffalo, NY 14240-9062. Include your complete name and address.

SPECIAL EXCERPT FROM

HARLEQUIN

Presents

*Does Charley Cazorla dare return to her husband's
bed? Does she even have a choice, when Raul is
offering a deal she really can't refuse…?*

*Read on for an exclusive excerpt of this stunning
new book by* **Michelle Smart**
THE PERFECT CAZORLA WIFE

"It won't happen again," she promised through ragged
breaths.

"I think you've told enough lies this past week, don't
you?"

Raul sat back down, waiting for the thunder beneath
his rib cage to abate.

How had things gotten out of hand so quickly?

He'd been taunting her, teasing her, asserting his
control, spelling out to her how much he held the upper
hand. He'd enjoyed it but had kept his mind firmly on the
seduction in hand.

She'd been the one to kiss him, a fact that, from the
look on her face, she regretted hugely.

She'd hooked her arm around his neck and his mind
had gone blank, desire overshadowing everything else.

The chemistry between them had always been explo-
sive, but that…

It had felt as if a coil locked in a too-tight box had
finally sprung free.

He'd been seconds away from taking her on the table.

She still stood there, her green eyes firing their hatred at him.

Whom did she hate the most? Him for compelling her back into his bed? Or herself for wanting it?

"So, *cariño*, do we have a deal?" He was gratified to hear his voice functioning as normal. He would *never* allow himself to show weakness in front of her. "The day care centre, signed, sealed, delivered and renovated in exchange for four months in my bed?"

Four months. That would surely be enough to get her out of his system once and for all.

Maybe it was fortuitous that she'd walked back into his life at this moment. He needed to move on, not just from the dissolution of their marriage but from the sexual hold she still held over him.

Her chin rose, her pretty nostrils flaring. "Yes. I accept your terms, but with one condition of my own—I won't be sharing your bed until the deeds of the building are in my hands."

"The building will be in the Cazorla name by the end of the week."

"Then you'll have to wait until then before you can touch me again."

"You are not in a position to make any demands, *cariño*."

Don't miss
THE PERFECT CAZORLA WIFE by Michelle Smart,
available August 2015 wherever
Harlequin Presents® books and ebooks are sold.

www.Harlequin.com

Copyright © 2015 by Harlequin Books, S.A.

HPEXP0715

HARLEQUIN
Presents®

A stunning conclusion to Carol Marinelli's latest
duet, ***Playboys of Sicily***, packed full of fiery passion,
dangerous temptation and heart-stopping excitement!

His until midnight…?

Losing her virginity to millionaire Matteo Santini came
at a high price for chambermaid Bella—unable to leave
Sicily with Matteo the next day, she lost her heart *and*
her one chance at happiness that night…

But now Matteo's back and more irresistible than ever!
Thrown together at Sicily's most exclusive wedding,
their sizzling attraction still burns bright, and as the
clock strikes midnight, it's clear the only way Bella will
be leaving the party is with Matteo—via his bed!

Find out what happens next in:

HIS SICILIAN CINDERELLA
AUGUST 2015

Stay Connected:

www.Harlequin.com

www.IHeartPresents.com

f /HarlequinBooks

y @HarlequinBooks

p /HarlequinBooks

HP13361

I ♥ Harlequin *Presents*

JUST CAN'T GET ENOUGH
OF THE ALPHA MALE?
Us either!

Come join us at **I Heart Presents** to hear the latest from your favorite Harlequin Presents authors and get special behind-the-scenes secrets of the Presents team!

With access to the latest breaking news and special promotions, **I Heart Presents** is *the* destination for all things Presents. Get up close and personal with the sexy alpha heroes who make your heart beat faster and share your love of these glitzy, glamorous reads with the authors, the editors and fellow Presents fans!

www.IHeartPresents.com

HPIHEART